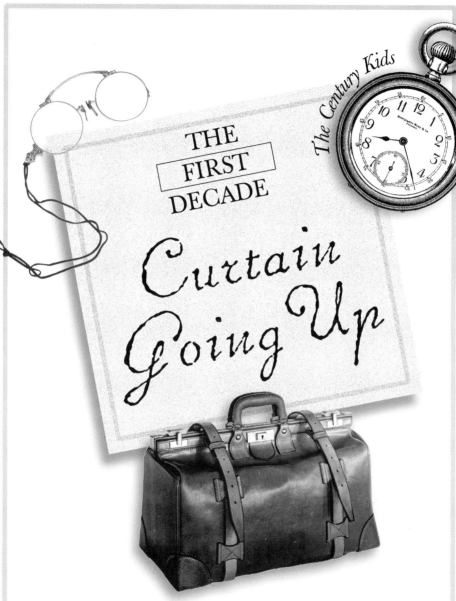

The Century Kids

THE
FIRST
DECADE

*Curtain
Going Up*

by Dorothy and Tom Hoobler

The Millbrook Press • *Brookfield, Connecticut*

Photographs courtesy of Corbis: pp. 3 (bottom), 154; Private collections: pp. 6, 13 (top), 15, 19, 21, 22, 30, 48, 51, 156 (Nell), 157 (Maud), 157 (Nick Woods); Culver Pictures, Inc.: pp. 7, 13 (bottom), 20, 49, 54, 85, 126; Underwood Photo Archives, Inc.: p. 18; Corbis/Bettmann: pp. 24, 61 (bottom), 71; North Wind Picture Archives: p. 33; The Granger Collection, New York: p. 61 (top); Brown Brothers: p. 120

In Memory of James P. Glenn

Hoobler, Dorothy.
The first decade: curtain going up / by Dorothy and Thomas Hoobler.
p.   cm.–(The century kids)
Summary: In the early years of the twentieth century, Peggy and her cousins Harry and Jack experience the excitement of belonging to a family of famous actors as they prepare to open a new theater with a family production of an original play.
ISBN 0–7613–1600–0 (lib. bdg.)
[1. Family life Fiction. 2. Cousins Fiction. 3. Actors and actresses Fiction. 4. Theater Fiction.] I. Hoobler, Thomas. II. Title.
III. Series: Hoobler, Dorothy. Century kids.
PZ7.H76227Fi   2000
[Fic]–dc21   99-37399   CIP

Published by The Millbrook Press, Inc.
2 Old New Milford Road
Brookfield, Connecticut 06804
www.millbrookpress.com

MS 2|01

54326

A Houseful of Smoke

DECEMBER 31, 1899

SITTING IN THE WINDOW SEAT WITH THE HEAVY green drapes pulled shut was like being in a little room all her own. Peggy rubbed the frost off the inside of a windowpane and peered out. The snow was falling harder now. In the moonlight she could see that the ground was already covered. If Jack and Harry arrived on time, they could all go sleigh riding tomorrow.

And they would, of course. It was a tradition. Twice each year, the Aldrich family gathered together in their big old house in Maine. Everybody in the theater world knew that you couldn't get the Aldriches to perform on New Year's Eve or the Fourth of July.

Peggy

Peggy strained to hear the sound of horses' hooves or the jingle of the harness bells on the carriage. It seemed like hours since Papa had gone to the train station to pick up Uncle Richard, Aunt Laura, and the boys.

But the only noises she could hear came from inside the house. An occasional clank echoed down the big chimney that ran through all three floors. Uncle Georgie was working on another invention. He said that fireplaces wasted too much heat and that he had found a way to make the logs burn longer. Nobody had too much faith in his ideas, but there wasn't anything you could do to stop him either.

Just inside the window seat was a vent that carried air up from the ground floor. If Peggy put her head close to it, she could hear the conversation in the room beneath this one. Down there, Mama and Grandma and Aunt Maud and Great-aunt Zena were sewing and talking about Mama's "confinement." That meant she was going to have a baby.

Whenever Peggy was around, they quickly changed the subject. As if she couldn't have guessed from the way Mama had gained weight and rested all the time. But Peggy wasn't quite sure just how the baby was going to get here, so she kept listening to the faint voices from below.

Most of all, though, she wanted to be awake at midnight, when the new century would begin. Oh, the grown-ups had all promised to wake her and the other children when that happened. But Peggy didn't think they really would. So after her younger cousins had fallen asleep upstairs, she tip-toed down and found her favorite hiding place here in Grandpa's study. She had brought a quilt, and wrapped it around her now. Warm and snug, she settled back to wait for the jingling bells. She would just close her eyes for a second.

⋆⇒◉⇐⋆

The next thing she knew, someone was calling her name—someone with a high, ghostly voice. And then the drapes parted and a fierce face appeared, lit only by a candle.

Peggy screamed and sat upright. The face broke into a smile, and a strong arm swooped Peggy up, quilt and all. The smell of brandy and pipe tobacco was enough to tell her who it was.

"Grandpa!" she scolded. "You frightened me!"

He laughed, and carried her over to the big leather couch against the wall. Gramps liked frightening people, and making them cry, or laugh, or shout with anger. He was the best actor in the nation,

Grandpa

everybody said. On all the walls of the study there were framed posters of plays he'd been in–Lionel Aldrich as the Count of Monte Cristo, Lionel Aldrich as Hamlet, Lionel Aldrich as Cyrano de Bergerac, and more.

These days, of course, he was retired and saved his acting tricks for his grandchildren. Mama said that theater producers kept asking him to take another role, but he always refused.

Setting Peggy down on the couch, he wagged his finger at her. "You would have frightened all of us," he said, "when we didn't find you in bed where you were supposed to be."

She rubbed her eyes. "Is it midnight yet?"

He took his pocket watch from the red watered-silk vest he always wore for the holidays. The lid snapped open and she could hear music playing. "Not quite eleven," he told her. "Another hour left in the old century. It's been a good one for me."

Grandpa looked away at something she couldn't see, remembering. Absentmindedly, he closed the cover and began to wind the watch.

"Can I wind it, Grandpa?" Peggy asked.

He gave her a strange look, and she was afraid that she'd said something wrong. But he took it off the chain and handed it to her. "Of course," he said. "Just be careful not to wind it too tightly."

It was too large for her to close her hand around. "It's heavy," she said.

He smiled. "It carries a lot of time on it. Just think, by the time it has to be wound again, a whole century will have gone by the boards."

Peggy turned the stem, feeling the clicks. "Can I open it and hear the music?" she asked.

"You know where the button is?"

"Right here." She pushed it, and the case popped open. It was cunning, she thought, as she heard the music start. "What song is it playing, Grandpa?"

"An old one," he said. His bright blue eyes twinkled in the candlelight. "Your grandmother and I danced to that song the night we first met."

As they listened, Peggy tried to imagine what Grandpa and Grandma had looked like. It was hard to think of them being young.

"When was that?" she asked.

Grandpa smoothed down his white hair. "Oh, sixty-two years ago." He reached out and snapped the watch cover shut.

"I wanted to listen to the end of the song," she protested.

He shook his head. "It's a little superstition of mine," he explained. "I never let it play all the way through." He winked at her. "Someday when this watch winds down, I will be gone too."

"Oh, Grandpa, don't say that."

His face turned sad, and she watched a tear fall from his eye.

Peggy clapped her hands. "You're *acting*, Grandpa, aren't you?"

He frowned, pretending to be cross now. "It's not very good acting if you can tell it's acting."

"But you made me feel sad anyway," she said. "How do you do that?"

"Do what?"

"Make yourself cry."

He smiled. "You'll learn."

Another loud clank came from the fireplace, and ashes fell down the chimney. The fire popped and sputtered.

Grandpa shook his head. "Georgie, Georgie," he said. "Why couldn't you have been content to be an actor like the rest of the family?"

"Uncle Georgie says that science will be the triumph of the twentieth century," Peggy said.

Grandpa snorted. "If so, I'm glad I won't see much of it. But I think he's wrong."

"Why?"

"Because everything that we need has already been invented. Mr. Thomas Edison has seen to that."

Peggy was quite surprised. "Why, Grandpa, I didn't think you liked Edison. You don't have electric lights in the house, you don't have—"

"There's a good reason for that," he told her.

"What is it?"

"I don't like electric lights."

Peggy giggled. "That's not a good reason."

He wiggled his bushy eyebrows at her. People said you could see those eyebrows in the back row of the balcony. She believed it.

"It's good enough for me," he told her.

He went over and sat behind the big old cherrywood desk in the middle of the room. "I own this house," he told her, "and a man's home—" He pointed to her, the way a prompter does in rehearsals.

"—is his castle," she finished. He nodded with approval.

"But Grandpa," Peggy said. "If everything has been invented, then there's no reason to go to school." She smiled mischievously.

Before Grandpa could answer, a louder chorus of clangs and bangs came from the chimney. Whatever Uncle Georgie was trying to invent, it seemed to make a lot of noise. Grandpa went to the fireplace and picked up a heavy iron poker. He rapped it against the bricks and shouted, "Stop that infernal racket at once!"

It seemed as if everything in the house went deadly silent. Nothing was wrong with Grandpa's voice, which had thrilled audiences for decades. There wouldn't be any need for anyone to wake the twins and little Freddy now, Peggy thought. They were probably sitting upright in bed, terrified.

Grandpa went back to the desk, smoothed his hair, and smiled at her. She could see he was trying to remember what she'd said. "School," he said, pleased with himself. "You must go to school because—"

There was a long pause.

Peggy broke the silence. "Grandma didn't go to school," she said.

He waved his hand. "Well, in those days people thought girls didn't need to." He raised a finger. "But we don't think that today. In the twentieth century, women will have to be educated."

"Papa and Uncle Richard and Aunt Maud didn't go to school, either, did they?"

Grandpa cleared his throat. "We were traveling around the country on tour," he explained. "They went with us, and we hired tutors for them."

She looked at him.

"Sometimes," he added.

"Mama told me that Uncle Georgie is the only one of your children who *ever* went to school," Peggy said.

The clanging started again.

"Well," said Grandpa, "we had to do something with him."

"I don't like school as much as traveling with Mama and Papa," Peggy said. In September, Mama had quit the stage because she was expecting the baby. Since then, she and Peggy had been living here at Grandpa's house. Peggy had been sent to school in the local village.

"Your cousins Harry and Jack are going to school," said Grandpa.

"That's because Aunt Laura wants them to be lawyers or doctors or something in an office," Peggy replied. "But I just want to go on the stage like Mama and Papa, and you."

"Your mother may not be going back to the stage," said Grandpa.

Peggy was surprised. But before she could reply, they heard footsteps on the stairway. The door opened, and Annie, the children's nanny, poked her head inside. She gave a cry of relief when she saw Peggy. "There you are!" Annie said. "When I didn't find you in your bed, I just nearly had a conniption."

Annie opened the door wider, and they could see she was carrying Freddy, the youngest of Peggy's cousins. The twins, Polly and Molly, peered out from behind her skirts.

Freddy

Molly

Polly

"Is it time for the New Year celebration, Annie?" asked Grandpa.

"Oh, no, sir. I had to bring the children down here because it's all filled with smoke upstairs."

"Smoke?"

Peggy pointed. "Look, Grandpa. There's smoke coming out of your fireplace, too."

"Blast," he said. "Georgie."

Suddenly they heard the sound of a bell downstairs. "Fire! Fire!" someone cried out. It sounded like Bridget, the housekeeper. She was ringing the big handbell she kept in the kitchen.

Annie gave a cry. "We'd better get out, sir." She turned and headed toward the stairs, dragging the children along.

"Go with her," Grandpa told Peggy. "Take your quilt. It's snowing outside."

"Grandpa, you have to come too!" she said.

"It's probably not a fire," he said. "But still—"

Peggy went to the door, wrapping the quilt around her. She turned and saw Grandpa at the far end of the room. "Hurry up!" she called to him. As she watched, he rolled up a corner of the carpet and tugged at a floorboard. It lifted upward and he pulled a small leather case from underneath the floor.

He hurried to the door and shooed Peggy out. As they ran down the stairs, he pressed his finger to his lips and said, "That's our secret, Peggy."

Before she could think about what he meant, they reached the main hallway. Everyone else in the house seemed to be standing there shouting at each other. "Stop ringing that bell!" Great-aunt Zena ordered Bridget, who paid no attention. Freddy and the twins were crying loudly, and Aunt Maud was helping Annie try to calm them. But Peggy's eyes went to her own mother, who was holding her stomach and looking very pale.

Grandmother put her arm around Mama and waved at Grandpa. "It's time," she called.

Peggy saw Grandpa's eyes widen. He took a deep breath, and then coughed, for the air down here was filled with smoke too.

"Out!" he shouted. Everyone else stopped talking and looked at him. "To the barn!" He pointed to the front door, and Peggy ran and opened it.

The First Noel or Nell?

DECEMBER 31, 1899–JANUARY 1, 1900

PEGGY WISHED SHE'D STOPPED TO PUT ON SHOES. The snow had soaked right through her slippers. Her feet were wet and cold, but at least there was dry straw here in the barn. Five horses were stabled inside (not counting two that Papa had taken with the carriage), and the heat from their bodies warmed the big room. Bridget brought a couple of oil lamps from the house. They threw shadows on the walls, and everybody's eyes reflected some of the flickering light. Inside their stalls, the horses started nickering and stamping, wondering why they'd been awakened. It would have been fun in a way—sort of like camping out, only with a horsey smell—except that Mama was about to have the baby.

Grandma and Great-aunt Zena took charge of that. They hustled Mama into an empty stall. Aunt Maud followed and closed the door. Peggy thought for a second and then went over. She lifted the latch and said, "I have a quilt for Mama." A hand reached out, took the quilt, and banged the stall door shut in her face.

Grandma

Well, Peggy thought, *that* wasn't such a bright idea. I lost the quilt and didn't get to see a thing. She put her head close to the door, trying to hear what was going on.

"Lionel," Grandma called from behind the door.

"Yes?" answered Grandpa.

"Distract the children," she commanded.

"Oh," he said. He looked from Peggy to the others, now tear-stained and sleepy. He glanced at Bridget and Annie, as if they might have a suggestion. They just looked worried. Uncle Nick, Aunt Maud's husband, shrugged and lit a cigar, the way he usually did.

Suddenly Bridget screamed and pointed toward the barn door. Peggy whirled around, thinking that maybe the baby was coming through there somehow. Instead, she saw a horrible black monster walking slowly toward her. He was covered with—

Oh. Covered with soot. It was—

"Georgie!" Grandpa called. "Stay away from the children. You'll get them dirty."

"I wondered where everybody had gone," said Georgie.

"Is the fire out?" asked Bridget.

"There was no fire," Georgie answered. He sounded irritated.

"But the smoke," Bridget continued.

"The invention worked perfectly fine," Georgie said with dignity. "More heat from the fireplaces stayed within the house. The only problem now is how to eliminate the smoke."

"That's what a chimney is for, Georgie," Grandpa said. "Now go back and clear ours out."

Georgie

"Oh, don't send him back in the house, sir," Bridget pleaded. "Think of the carpets."

"I've cleared the chimney already," Georgie said.

"And there's no fire?" Bridget asked him.

"Except in the fireplaces," he said.

"Then if you don't mind," Bridget said to Grandpa, "I'll go and open the windows."

"You can't do that," Georgie said. "You'll let out all the heat."

"Go ahead, Bridget," said Grandpa. Just then, a brief cry came from the stall behind Peggy. It frightened her, because it sounded like Mama.

"Adele!" called Grandpa. "Should Bridget bring boiling water?"

"Of course not," came Grandma's voice from behind the door. "But we could use a sheet and blankets."

"Right away, ma'am," called Bridget.

As she headed outside, they heard the hoofbeats that Peggy had been waiting for. She ran out, not caring that her bare feet sank into the snow again. There was Papa! He hopped down from the driver's seat of the carriage. "Peggy!" he said. "What on earth?"

Papa

"Everybody's in the barn, Papa," she said. "And Mama's having the baby!"

He stared for a second, and then ran inside. Uncle Richard, Aunt Laura, Jack, and Harry slowly got out of the carriage. Uncle Richard, as always, looked handsome and heroic, as if he'd come to save the day. That was the kind of role he always played on stage. He turned his head when he spoke to you, so you could see his profile. In real life, as the whole family knew, he needed Aunt Laura to tell him what to do.

"Why is everybody down *here?*" Aunt Laura asked. "There's no one to take our luggage inside."

"The house is filled with smoke," Peggy told her.

Jack and Harry laughed and poked each other. "What did Uncle Georgie do now?" Jack asked.

Richard

"Wait till you see him," Peggy giggled. She was so glad Jack and Harry were here that she hugged them both. They looked cute in their Pemberton caps and school blazers. "You're in your nightie," Jack protested. "Why are you running around in the snow without shoes?"

They all went into the barn. Aunt Laura shrieked when she saw Uncle Georgie. "Get away from me!" she cried, even though he wasn't even close to her. She was, as always, dressed in the latest fashion. Her green dress with black trim was set off by a large hat decorated with ostrich feathers. Uncle Georgie tried to move farther away, but there was no place to go. Aunt Laura pointed to the door. "Go to the lake and clean yourself off!" she commanded. Peggy was about to say that the lake had frozen over, but she decided Uncle Georgie could find that out himself.

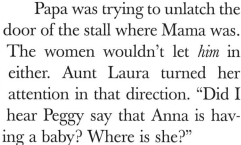

Laura

Papa was trying to unlatch the door of the stall where Mama was. The women wouldn't let *him* in either. Aunt Laura turned her attention in that direction. "Did I hear Peggy say that Anna is having a baby? Where is she?"

Grandpa gestured in the direction of the stall. "In there?" Aunt Laura said, with her hand to her throat. "In the *barn*? What's going on here?"

"Hush up, Laura," came Grandma's voice. "We're doing just fine."

Aunt Laura stared at the closed stall door. Grandma was one person she didn't argue with. So she turned to her husband. "Richard, we're leaving."

Grandpa stepped forward and put his hand on her arm. "Don't be in such a hurry, Laura. We have a lovely midnight supper planned. We'll all see the new century in together."

She looked around. "You can't have all these children here," she said.

"Well, two of them are yours," Grandpa said. "Fine boys, too."

"I don't mean that," she began, but Grandpa interrupted her.

"Why don't we all sing?" he said. "You have a lovely voice, and we'll all join in."

Aunt Laura was indeed proud of her singing, Peggy knew. It just took her a moment to get used to the idea of singing in a barn. Grandpa went on smoothly. "Let's sing a Christmas carol. Everybody likes those. 'The First Noel.' Does everybody know the words? Peggy? Harry? Jack?"

The three of them nodded. "All right then," Grandpa said. "Ready, Laura? You take the lead, and we'll follow."

The singing wasn't as good as it might have been if they had rehearsed, but after a few bars even Polly and Molly were joining in. Peggy thought she heard Mama cry out again, but Aunt Laura raised her voice an octave when that happened. Freddy seemed to be soothed by the song and went back to sleep in Annie's arms. Papa was the only one who didn't seem to be contributing as well as he might.

Of course, Peggy remembered hearing Great-aunt Zena declare that men were absolutely useless to have around when the baby came. It didn't seem fair, Peggy thought, that they couldn't do something to help.

All at once, they heard the clatter of more hoofbeats. Through the doorway, Peggy could see the fire-tanker wagon from town clatter through the gates. Half a dozen men clung to the sides, and more followed on horseback.

Inwardly, Peggy groaned when she saw that the chief of the volunteer firefighters was Mr. Pomeroy. He was the owner of the general store in town, and for some reason he detested actors. His

son Marshall was the main reason why Peggy hated going to the local school. Marshall tormented her constantly.

Grandpa and the others went right on singing as the fire tanker rolled to a stop. Finally, after finishing the verse, Grandpa walked to where the men were unrolling the big hose, getting ready to squirt water on the fire.

"No need, no need for that!" Grandpa called to them.

Mr. Pomeroy turned around. He was a thin man with a black handlebar mustache that looked too large for his face. "What do you mean, no need? The telephone operator at central station sounded the fire alarm. She reported that there was a fire here."

Carrying blanket and sheets, Bridget approached from the house in time to hear. "Oh, sir. I was the one who used the telephone to spread the alarm."

Grandpa looked annoyed. Peggy knew that he had allowed a telephone in the house only because it was supposed to be useful in emergencies. "But it was just a mistake," Grandpa said to Mr. Pomeroy.

Mr. Pomeroy looked suspiciously at all the Aldriches standing in the barn. "Then why have you all fled the house?"

"There was smoke inside, due to a—a clogged chimney," Grandpa said.

"Did I hear singing when we arrived?" asked Mr. Pomeroy.

"We were singing to calm my sister-in-law," broke in Aunt Laura. "She is delivering her baby."

Mr. Pomeroy's eyeballs looked as if they were going to fall out. "Delivering her baby? Now?"

Just then, another cry came from the barn. A different one. Not Mama, but a baby's crying. Peggy looked over at Baby Freddy. He was still asleep, so that must mean—

"I think you've become a father again, Bill!" Uncle Richard slapped Papa on the back. "Congratulations!"

Peggy heard the music coming from Grandpa's watch. He snapped it shut and announced, "It's just past midnight! This must be the first child born in the twentieth century!"

"You should call him Noel!" piped up Jack. And with that, he and Harry started to sing again. The rest of the Aldriches joined in for another chorus of 'The First Noel.'

Mr. Pomeroy didn't seem to share their joy. Peggy heard him tell one of the other volunteers, "The whole bunch of them must have been drinking. You know, even the women and children are in the theater. None of them are decent."

Grandpa overheard the remark, too, and his eyebrows jumped up and down. "I beg your pardon, sir. You may insult me all you like, but gentlemen don't cast slurs on ladies."

Mr. Pomeroy looked taken aback at this. But when some of the other volunteers chuckled at his distress, he pointed a finger at Grandpa. "You've taken us away from our own family celebrations," he said. "All for a false alarm."

Grandpa nodded. "So we have. To make amends, I invite you all to join us inside. The smoke must be nearly gone by now, and we have refreshments."

Bridget looked alarmed. Peggy knew why. She hadn't prepared for ten additional guests.

Fortunately Mr. Pomeroy's reply was to turn and tell the volunteers, "We're wasting our time here, fellows. Let's go home."

But the other men hesitated, looking wistfully at the house. They were curious about what the Aldrich mansion looked like inside.

It was Aunt Maud who provided the excuse they needed. She came walking up from the barn and asked, "Did you bring a stretcher on that fire-wagon?"

"Yes, ma'am," one of the men said. "In case of an injury."

"We could use some help bringing my sister-in-law up to the house," Aunt Maud told him.

All at once, nine of the volunteers sprang into action. The only one who wasn't eager to help was, of course, Mr. Pomeroy. That was all right, because it only took two men to carry the stretcher, and the rest just wanted to go inside the house.

Aunt Maud turned to Papa. "Anna's doing fine, Bill. And you have a fine new little girl."

Papa blinked. "Oh," he said. "We thought this one would be a boy."

"Tough luck, Bill," said Uncle Richard. "I guess we named her too soon."

Papa smiled. "Oh, no," he said. "Anna and I would just as soon have a girl. And if we can't call her Noel, we'll call her . . . Nell!"

"Three cheers for Nell, then!" shouted Harry, and the shouts of "hip, hip, hooray!" echoed through the pines.

"And another three for the twentieth century," Uncle Richard proposed. It sounded strange, Peggy thought, as they all shouted. She wondered whether the twentieth century would be as good as Grandpa said the last one was.

THREE

Grandpa's Plan

JANUARY 1, 1900

PEGGY USUALLY WAS UP BEFORE ANYBODY ELSE, but that New Year's Day, Annie had to wake her. She'd been up too late the night before. "You'd better hurry," Annie called, "or you won't get any breakfast."

Peggy shut her eyes firmly. She knew that she could always persuade Bridget to give her something to eat, no matter what time it was. But when she tried to pull her quilt up, she found that it had been replaced by a woolen blanket.

Then she remembered. "I gave the quilt to Mama," she said aloud. All the other memories came rushing back, too.

Jumping out of bed, she asked Annie, "Where's the baby?"

"I have her in my room for now," Annie replied. "Just for a few weeks, till she's ready to sleep in the nursery with Freddy."

"Can I see her?"

"If you're quiet. She's asleep."

Peggy tiptoed down the hall. When she peeked in the door to Annie's room, Mama was there in her nightgown, too—a new flannel one with pink embroidery. She was leaning over the baby's crib, but looked up when Peggy appeared.

"Are you all right, Mama?" Peggy said.

Mama

"Oh yes, dear. I'll be fine."

Peggy studied her face. Mama looked just as beautiful as ever. She had even put her hair up, and her blue eyes sparkled.

"I wish I'd been there when you had the baby."

Mama smiled. "There wasn't enough room in that horse stall, I'm afraid."

"We sang to make you feel better. Did you hear?"

"Yes. It was very nice."

Peggy looked down at the baby. It was still wrapped tightly in a blanket. "When do they let it out?" she asked.

"Let it out?"

"You know, unwrap it."

Mama laughed. "It's to keep her warm."

"Mama," said Peggy, "will you have to take care of the baby for a long time?"

Mama looked puzzled. "Well, till she's grown up, I guess."

"Really? Is there something the matter with her?"

"No, dear, she's fine." Mama thought about it. "But that doesn't mean I don't love you," she said. "I'll still take care of you, too."

"But I meant how long will it be till you go back on stage?"

"Oh, I see," Mama said.

"When I was born, you and Papa just took me along, didn't you?"

"We did, yes. But you were an easy baby," Mama said, remembering with a smile. "We just put you in a trunk."

Peggy looked into the crib. "She could fit into a trunk without any trouble. She doesn't look like a hard baby."

Mama laughed. "Well, this time I may stay here for a while."

"I don't want to stay here. Grandpa wants us to stay *forever*."

"Why, Peggy! I'm surprised at you. Don't you like it here?"

31

"Not as much as traveling with you and Papa."

"Your grandparents have invited us to stay for as long as we want. And now that you're in school, I thought—"

"That's just it!" Peggy said. "I hate that school."

She was sorry she said it, because it put a sad look on Mama's face. Fortunately, Annie arrived then, and told Mama that she ought to be in bed resting. Peggy went back to her own room and got dressed. Downstairs, she could smell something good cooking.

It turned out to be hotcakes with sausages and maple syrup. "I expected you earlier," Bridget said as Peggy wolfed down her first mouthful. "You're usually up before the sun."

Peggy couldn't reply. She was trying to keep the maple syrup from running down her chin.

"You just missed the boys," Bridget added. "They went to hitch up the sleigh."

Peggy rapped her fist on the table. She swallowed and asked, "Have they gone yet?"

Bridget looked out the window. "They're bringing the sleigh out of the barn just now. You can get someone else to take you out this afternoon."

It was an agonizing decision. Peggy looked longingly at the hotcakes. Then she jumped up, grabbed two of them and used them to sop up a puddle of syrup on her plate. Bridget shouted when she saw what she was doing, but Peggy ran toward the coat rack, hotcakes dripping stickily over her hand.

Outside, with one arm in a coat sleeve and the other still holding the hotcakes, she ran toward the barn shouting. The boys reined in the horse and gave her a lift up into the sleigh.

"Ugh, you're sticky," Jack said, wiping his hand on his coat.

"It's syrup," she said.

They let her snuggle between them on the seat. Harry held the reins, but they were hardly

necessary. Old Vixen would take the sleigh down the path to the lake road without being urged. Her head bobbed up and down, steam coming out of her nostrils, as if she enjoyed the crisp air as much as the children did.

"We thought you would sleep in today," Jack told Peggy. "You were still up last night when we went to bed."

"I didn't feel like sleeping," she said. "I was too excited."

Harry nudged Peggy and said, "Hey, you know we've lived in two centuries now?"

She smiled. They had heard that joke a hundred times at the party. The volunteers had kept repeating it.

"You know," said Jack, "I think those people from the town were disappointed."

"Oh, no, they stayed for more than an hour," Peggy replied. "Bridget brought out eggnog and three kinds of cake."

"But they really thought they were going to see something . . . I don't know . . . *scandalous* in Grandpa's house," Jack said. "You could tell."

"They think actors are like criminals," Peggy said.

"Not Father," Harry broke in. "Everybody loves him. Whenever he's in a play, the theater is packed." Harry was his father's biggest fan. His goal in life was to be just like the characters his father played—brave, daring, and bold.

"That's in the big cities," Peggy said. "In this town, they haven't got a theater. Nobody ever saw a real actor before Grandpa and Grandma built their house. You don't know what it's like. When I went to school here, the kids treated me like I had a disease."

The sleigh reached the lake, shimmering and frozen all the way across. On the other side was the town. "Shall we take the sleigh across the lake?" Harry asked. He shook the reins, urging Vixen to go onto the ice.

"No!" Jack and Peggy both shouted together.

Harry pointed. "Look, there are skaters out in the middle."

"That's not the same as a sleigh and horse," Peggy said.

Shrugging, Harry let Vixen go the way she wanted, on the narrow road that led around the shore. The steel runners of the sleigh made singing noises against the hard-packed snow and ice.

"That man who rode off rather than come into the house—" Jack recalled. "He was the worst one." Jack was the younger brother, by a year. He and Peggy were the same age. But although Harry was bigger and stronger, Peggy thought Jack was the clever one. He understood things that Harry didn't.

"Don't tell me," Peggy said. "That's Mr. Pomeroy. His son Marshall is always doing something to annoy me. He put a frog in my desk."

Both Harry and Jack snickered at that.

"I didn't find it funny," Peggy said. "And he was the one who said actors weren't respectable people."

"We have fellows at our school like that," Jack said. "They try to bully you and things."

"You have to stand up to them," Harry added. "If you don't it just gets worse."

"But he's old," said Peggy. "He's fourteen, the oldest boy in the school."

"Maybe he'll leave school in the spring," Jack suggested, "to work on the farm."

"His father owns the general store in town," Peggy replied glumly. "He thinks Marshall should go to college."

"There was a boy at our school," Jack told her, "who used to kick me under the desk whenever I stood up to recite."

"I offered to beat him up," Harry said, "but Jack wouldn't let me."

"Then *you* would have gotten in trouble," Jack said.

"I can't beat up Marshall," Peggy said.

"Jack didn't beat this boy up either," said Harry. "He did worse."

"What did you do?" asked Peggy.

"Nothing really," Jack said with a smile.

"Jack sprinkled something on his clothes," Harry said. "It smelled so bad nobody could stand to be around him."

"What was it?" Peggy asked.

"They had to burn his clothes and make him take a bath in lye soap," Harry added, rolling his eyes. "It was *horrible*."

Jack laughed. "Nobody knew it was me."

"Oh, he knew," Harry said. "He stopped kicking you, didn't he?"

"He was worried because he only had one other school uniform," Jack said with an evil grin.

"Could you make some of that for me?" Peggy asked.

"I don't know," Jack replied. "I need sulfur and some other things."

"I'll bet Uncle Georgie could get whatever you need," she said.

"Probably," Jack said. "But you never know what will happen once he gets started on an idea."

"We might end up having to air out the whole house again," Harry said. "Only this time it would be worse than smoke."

The wind began to rise, sending a chill through them. After a while, they turned the sleigh and went back to the house. They unhitched old Vixen, rubbed her down, and put her back in the barn.

As they went inside the house, they heard noises from the sitting room. It sounded like Grandpa shouting while Aunt Laura sang. Or really, in a strange way, like *two* Aunt Lauras singing. "It must be the present we brought for Grandpa," Jack explained.

"I *knew* that he wouldn't like it," said Harry.

As they peeked through the door, Grandpa saw them and called them inside. "Here, now, Peggy. You have some sense. They can't call *you* old-fashioned, can they?"

"What's the matter, Grandpa?" she asked.

"Look at this gadget here," he said, gesturing toward a wooden box that had a shiny black horn—shaped like a dunce cap—lying on top of it. As she came closer, Peggy saw that there was a crank sticking out of the side of the box.

Uncle Georgie was standing next to the box. "It's a Gramophone," he said, the same way a normal person might say, "It's the answer to all my hopes and dreams." Of course, he talked the same way about his own inventions, too.

"Mama made a recording of her latest song," Jack said. "The machine plays it, you see."

"I don't understand," said Peggy. "We heard Aunt Laura singing when we came in."

"And this machine sounds nothing at all like her," said Grandpa.

"I was singing along with the recording, just to show how much alike they were," Aunt Laura said. "Go ahead, Georgie. Wind it up and let the children hear it."

Uncle Georgie turned the crank and made some adjustments to the machinery. Out of the shiny black horn came some noise that sounded, to Peggy, like very faint music. Then a voice, singing, "She's only a bird in a gilded cage—"

Peggy realized that the singer in the machine must be Aunt Laura. It *was* a very cunning invention, she thought. At the same time, however, she agreed with Grandpa.

"The Gramophone is wonderful," Peggy said, "but I'd much rather hear you sing outside of a box, Aunt Laura."

Grandpa roared with laughter, and Aunt Laura couldn't hide her smile. "Very well said, Peggy," said Grandpa.

Uncle Georgie didn't agree. "The Gramophone is only in its infancy," he said. "The sound quality will improve. Someday, people won't go to concert halls or theaters, because every home will have one of these."

Grandpa's eyebrows flashed up and down like angry caterpillars. "Balderdash!" he said.

"Lionel, the children are present," warned Grandma.

Grandpa stood and struck a dramatic pose. "I won't listen to anyone—particularly a son of mine—predict the death of the theater!" he said. He had such a wonderful voice, Peggy thought.

He turned and swept his arm grandly around the room. "I've come to a realization," he went on. "Those townspeople who were here last night made me see that I have been—" He paused for suspense and to make sure everybody was listening. "A fool!" he concluded.

Of course, everybody chimed in at once to assure him that he wasn't a fool, not at all.

He raised his finger for silence. "I have been unaware of my neighbors."

Well, that much was true, Peggy thought. If you called the people of the town neighbors even though the nearest house was a mile away. Grandpa only passed through the town on the way to the railroad station.

"And they thought me a strange old bird, a solitary recluse, a werewolf howling at the moon."

"Lionel, they were just curious," said Grandma.

"What's a recluse?" asked Harry, but no one answered.

"One of them said that actors were indecent drunkards," Grandpa went on.

"Is that what a recluse is?"

"I never heard anyone say that, I'm sure," Grandma said.

"It was Mr. Pomeroy," Peggy said, trying to remember if that was exactly what he'd said.

"Well, it was a silly thing to say," Grandma said.

"At any rate, I've come to a decision," announced Grandpa.

"I hope you'll tell us what it is," said Grandma, "because Bridget is ringing her bell, and since the room isn't filled with smoke, that means lunch is ready."

Grandpa folded his arms. "I'm going to build a theater," he said.

"Where?" asked Uncle Richard.

"Right here, of course," replied Grandpa.

"I knew he couldn't stay retired," said Great-aunt Zena. Everyone was talking about Grandpa's plan as they went into the dining room. Peggy was the only one who knew what it really meant, however. He *does* want us all to stay here forever, she thought.

March 9, 1900

Dear Jack:

I am not going to need that powder after all. I mean the stuff that you used to make a bully smell bad. I guess you haven't sent it because maybe it would make the mail stink too much.

Marshall Pomeroy is still mean to me. The other day he said that girls with red hair were ugly. I asked Grandpa if that were true. It made him angry. Mama told me later that Grandma had red hair when she was young. Did you know that? That must be where I get mine.

Anyway, Grandpa decided I should stay at home and have a tutor. Who do you think the tutor is? Great-aunt Zena! I'd rather have Uncle Georgie tutor me. At least I would learn something fun. He has been working on a new invention, of course!

He was inspired when the volunteer firefighters arrived on New Year's Eve. Uncle Georgie thinks he could use hot-air balloons to carry buckets of water over a fire. He says the big problem is getting the water to pour out onto the fire. But you can imagine that getting the balloon to go up in the air hasn't been so easy, either.

I do have another teacher. His name is Michael. He's actually Annie's brother. She saved the money to pay for his ship ticket to come here from Ireland. Grandpa gave him a job as a groom at the stables, and guess what? Mama said Michael could teach me to ride! Hooray! I wanted to ride Shakespeare, the big stallion, but Michael said I have to start learning on Vixen.

Papa is on tour with a production of <u>East Lynne</u>. To cheer me up, he sent me a Brownie camera and told me to take pictures of Mama and the baby. I am going to make a photograph album.

Oh, and Grandpa hasn't forgotten about building a theater. A man came to the house last week. He designs buildings. He is an arkatek architect. I asked Great-aunt Zena how to spell that, and she said I should be studying now, so I must close. Grandpa had a special room equipped as a classroom, and here I am.

Write back soon. Tell me if you played any more tricks on your classmates. I don't have any.

Your cousin,
Peggy

FOUR

Thief on the Train

JULY 2, 1902

"I THINK MOTHER WOULD JUST AS SOON STAY IN New York," said Jack.

Harry was looking out the window of the train. He had opened it, and a brisk breeze swept through as they sped along. It was a hot day, and the train was crowded with passengers going somewhere for the holiday. "Oh, she can't do that," Harry said.

"Why do you think she sent us up to Maine by ourselves?"

"It's just that they have a performance tonight. She and Father will come up tomorrow."

"I wouldn't be surprised if they didn't," said Jack.

Jack

"They have to come," Harry said. "The Aldriches all have to come to Grandpa's house twice a year."

"Mother isn't really an Aldrich," Jack pointed out.

"She is by marrying Father," Harry replied. "Anyway, *he* will come, and bring her along."

Jack wondered if that were true. The conductor came down the aisle and asked for their tickets. As he punched them, he said, "Are you boys traveling by yourselves?"

"Yes, we are," Jack said. "But don't worry, I can take care of him." It was an old joke. Even though Jack was only a year younger, Harry had always been much taller and stronger.

The conductor smiled. "I just wondered if you knew you don't have to change trains in Boston," he said. "This one is going straight through to Portland."

"We know, thanks," said Jack.

"You boys headed to camp in Maine?"

"No, we're visiting relatives," Jack said.

"Our father is Richard Aldrich," Harry blurted out. Jack cringed.

The conductor recognized the name, of course. You could see his face change. "Is that right? I saw him on the stage once in Buffalo. I'll

48

never forget it. He was one of the Three Muske-teers, and he jumped out of a window that must have been fifteen feet high!"

"That's nothing," said Harry. "You should have seen him in *The Knights of the Round Table.*"

"He's in a play in New York right now, isn't he?"

"Yes, with Mother," Harry said. "*Captain Jinks of the Horse Marines.*"

"I would think you'd spend your holi-day with them."

"They're coming up later. We're all going to my grandfather's house."

"Your grandfather? Is that Lionel Aldrich?"

Harry nodded. "That's right."

"Oh, they say he was the best of them all." The conductor's voice lowered. "I thought he was dead."

"No, he's just retired."

"Well, if you boys get hungry, let me know before you come to the dining car." He winked. "I'll have the cook fix you something special."

After the conductor had moved farther on, Jack said, "I wish you wouldn't tell everybody that we're related to Father."

"Why not?" asked Harry.

"It's . . . embarrassing. Listen to him. He's telling everybody in the car that we're Richard Aldrich's sons."

49

"So what?"

"I don't like people staring at me."

"It doesn't bother me," said Harry. "When I grow up, I'm going to be like Father."

"You mean go on the stage?" Once, Jack remembered, their parents had arranged for Harry to take a role in a play that needed a little boy. When Harry had to speak his one line—which was "Hooray for General Grant!"—he had frozen and forgotten it.

"No," Harry said. He looked out the window, and then back at Jack. "I'm going to do heroic and brave things."

"Harry," said Jack, "Father only *plays* heroes on the stage."

"I don't care," Harry said stubbornly. "I'm going to be just like him."

"It would be better to do something else," Jack said.

"Like what?"

"Well, get into business or science, for instance."

"Those are boring things," Harry said.

Jack decided there was no use arguing with Harry. He was just like the conductor, and practically everybody else who'd ever seen Father. Father looked like a hero. He acted like a hero.

But it was all acting, just the same.

At any rate, the conductor kept his word. When Harry and Jack went to the dining car, the waiter brought a whole roast beef to their table. He sliced off as many pieces as they asked for, gave them all the mashed potatoes they wanted, and followed that up with ice cream and chocolate cake.

Harry poked Jack as they went back to their seat in the passenger car. "You still think I shouldn't have told the conductor who we were?" he asked with a grin.

Jack didn't say anything, but he thought, It isn't who *we* are, but who our father plays on stage.

Back in their seats, Harry curled up and went to sleep. Jack took out a

Harry

book about science and started to read. It wasn't boring to him. He felt that science was the only real thing there was. It got right to the heart of what the world was all about. But the more he read, the more he realized he had to learn.

Right now, for example, the wind blowing through the window was gently lifting his brother's hair. Harry wouldn't have noticed even if he'd been awake. But Jack knew that there was something in the wind—something invisible. Atoms. You couldn't see them, but they were there in the air all around them. That was why Harry's hair rose up. Atoms pushed it.

He turned the page of his book and found a letter from Peggy. He had tucked it in there last week when it arrived, and forgotten about it. She wrote Jack a lot, more often than he wrote back. It was not that he didn't care. He liked reading about what was going on at Grandpa's house. He just didn't have as much to tell her.

He opened the envelope. There was a photograph inside, one that Peggy had taken. Jack laughed. It showed Uncle Georgie aiming a rifle at one of the hot-air balloons he'd sent up in the air. He was trying to use them to drop water on fires. He'd been at it now for over a year. The only progress was that the balloons had gotten bigger. Once Georgie managed to drop water on a line of clothes that were hung out to dry. Another time he scored a direct hit on Great-aunt Zena while she was working in the flower garden. Meanwhile, the fires he had set in order to put them out had gotten out of control. He had burned down a tool shed and nearly started a forest fire as well.

Jack read on. The new theater was still being built. Grandpa had decided to have electric lights installed after all. But the project turned out to be bigger than anybody expected. It wouldn't be finished until next year.

The last part of the letter made Jack laugh out loud. Uncle Georgie would probably meet them at the train station. "He won't be in the carriage, though," Peggy wrote. "Now he has an automobile."

When Harry woke up, Jack told him. "What kind is it?" Harry asked.

"She doesn't say."

Harry reached for the letter. "Let me see. She must have."

"You think I can't read?"

"But that's the most important thing!" Harry said. "It could be a Stanley, or a Winton, or a Haynes, or even an Oldsmobile."

"He wouldn't have an Oldsmobile," said Jack. "They're too popular."

"Yes, you're right. He probably has some strange kind we never heard of."

"Or made one himself." They laughed. That would be most likely.

Quite a few people left the train when it reached Boston, but nearly as many boarded it. Like Harry and Jack, they seemed to be headed for Maine, where the weather was often cooler. The train sat in the station for at least half an hour. Finally, the conductor called out "All aboard!" and they started to move again.

The last part of the trip always seemed the slowest, even though it was shorter on the map.

They were tired of sitting in the car, and too restless to sleep. Jack went back to his science book, but Harry stood up to stretch his legs. He walked toward the back of the train, enjoying the feeling of the car rocking gently from side to side.

A few people looked up at him as he passed, but most were reading newspapers or looking out the window or sleeping. In the last seat, by the window, there was a red-faced man who had loosened his tie and removed his coat. His head rested on the seatback and his eyes were closed. His suit jacket was lying folded on the empty seat next to him.

As Harry watched in surprise, a hand reached across the aisle from the seat on the other side. As quick as a hummingbird, it slipped inside the coat and brought out something. Harry blinked. It had happened so fast, he wasn't even sure what had been taken. It looked like a leather wallet.

Then a man's head rose up from behind the opposite seat. He was young and well-dressed, wearing a blue blazer with a boater, or flat straw hat. He had a pleased expression on his face until he noticed Harry staring at him. Then his grayish eyes narrowed and he gave Harry a look that sent a chill down his spine.

The Thief

Just as swiftly as he had moved earlier, the man left his seat and moved up the aisle toward Harry. Harry put up his arms, thinking that he ought to try and stop him. But the man came forward till his face was right up near Harry's. He had a sandy-colored mustache and smelled of shaving lotion. He roughly pushed Harry out of the way and continued up the aisle.

Harry was dumbfounded. He wanted to cry out, "Stop, thief!" the way that heroes always did in plays or stories. Nobody else had noticed what had happened. None of the other passengers even glanced at the man. Harry tried to cry out, but his voice wouldn't work.

He turned to look at the sleeping man. Still sleeping. Harry took a step forward and tapped him on the arm. His eyes opened and he looked startled, then annoyed. "What's the matter?" he said.

"I think . . . " Harry began, "is something missing from your jacket?"

The man stared at him. Then he reached for his jacket and checked the pockets. "Why, yes!" he said. "My wallet's gone." He grabbed hold of Harry's arm, angry now, his face even redder. "What did you do with it?"

"It wasn't me," Harry explained quickly. "That man . . . " he started to say. He turned and pointed, but the thief had already gone through to the next car.

"What man?"

"There was a man in a blue blazer," Harry explained. "He took your wallet, and then went up the aisle."

"Why didn't you *stop* him?" the second man said. Unlike Harry, he had no trouble raising his voice, and people were starting to turn around in their seats.

"I wasn't sure . . . " Harry said helplessly. Then he had an idea. "Let's follow him," he said. "He can't have left the train."

They hurried up the aisle and opened the door to the next car. Jack looked up from his book as they passed him. "What's going on, Harry?" he asked. Nobody answered.

Harry's heart sank as he scanned the car and saw nobody in the aisle except the conductor. But maybe the thief was in one of the seats. With the angry man still following, Harry started looking at every passenger.

The conductor blocked their way halfway up the car. "Is something the matter?" he said.

"My wallet's been stolen," the man explained. "This boy says he saw someone take it." Harry glanced at him. The way he said it made it sound like maybe he thought Harry was lying.

"I did! I just wasn't . . . "

"What did he look like?" the conductor asked.

"He was . . . young," Harry said, "and good-looking. He was wearing a blue blazer and a boater."

The conductor looked around. Harry could see that several passengers were wearing exactly the same outfit. "But I'd know him if I saw him," Harry said.

Checking his watch, the conductor said, "We're almost to Portsmouth. The train will stop there, and I can't hold people on board if they want to get off."

Harry ran along now, just glancing into each seat. With the conductor and the man following, he crossed into yet another car. By this time, the train had started to slow down. Some people were already standing and reaching for their luggage in the overhead racks.

It was hard to get through the aisle now. There was a hiss and a jolt as the train's air brakes kicked in. Harry turned back, facing the conductor. "I've got to get off and see if the thief leaves the train."

"You're not going anywhere," said the man whose wallet had been stolen. "I want him searched," he said to the conductor.

Uncertainly, the conductor looked back and forth. "Why, this boy is the son of Richard Aldrich," he said.

"I don't care if he's J.P. Morgan's son," the man said. "I want to make sure he hasn't got my wallet."

Harry was angry now. "You're letting the thief get away!" The train had stopped now, and people were heading for the doors at either end of the car.

"Better the one I've seen than the one I didn't," said the man smugly.

Harry turned his pockets inside out—jacket and pants. The only things he had were a handkerchief, a jackknife, some pocket change, and a five-dollar bill his father had given him when they left.

The man still wasn't satisfied. "What about that boy we passed in the other car?" he asked the conductor. "He said something to this one."

"They're brothers," said the conductor.

"He could have slipped the other one my wallet," the man insisted.

So they went back and Harry had to ask Jack to turn his pockets out.

"What's going on?" Jack asked.

"I'll explain later," Harry said.

Jack decided to joke about it, unfortunately. "Just as long as they don't look in the suitcase," he said in a low voice that made him sound just like a criminal. He was imitating an actor who'd been in a play with Father.

That meant, of course, that they had to search the suitcase, too, as well as all of Jack's pockets.

And that was why Jack and Harry weren't saying very much to each other when the train reached Kennebunk.

FIVE

A Challenge

MOST OF THEIR ANGER DISAPPEARED WHEN THEY stepped off the train and saw Uncle Georgie waiting for them. For once, he looked normal. He wore white duck pants, a shirt with light blue and white stripes, and a small blue bow tie. The only thing that made him look different from the other people on the platform was a dark blue cap and the pair of goggles that hung around his neck.

"You really have an automobile?" Jack asked.

"Sure do," Uncle Georgie said. "I started reading about what the Duryea brothers had done, and–"

"You didn't get a Duryea?" Harry asked. The boys at school didn't think much of Duryea autos.

59

"No, come on and see," Uncle Georgie said.

Jack shook his head. He was sure Uncle Georgie had built something idiotic that would break down on the way to Grandpa's house.

Then they saw it. The sun was setting, but there was still enough light to reflect off the gleaming black and red carriage. No, that was wrong. It looked like a carriage—a small one, without a top—but there were no shafts to hitch a horse to it.

Jack looked at the stylish curved dashboard. "It's an Oldsmobile," he said in a reverent tone.

Then Harry yelled it: "Hurrah! You got an Oldsmobile!"

They ran over and touched it. The polished wooden body of the automobile felt smooth and strong as they slid their hands around it. They looked underneath and saw the engine that they knew had the power of seven horses.

"All right, now who's going to sit on the back?" Uncle Georgie asked.

Harry and Jack looked at the seat and then at each other. "It faces the rear!" Jack pointed out unnecessarily. "You could only see where you've come from."

"I'm the oldest," Harry announced as he pulled himself up onto the front seat.

"But I'm the toughest," Jack said as he grabbed Harry's arm and tried to pull him down.

"Boys, wait," said Uncle Georgie, waving his arms. Fighting always made him upset. "You can

both sit there if we squeeze together. Put on the goggles, though, to keep the dust from the road from getting in your eyes."

They found two more pairs of goggles under the front seat. Laughing, they put them on and stared at each other. "You look like a raccoon," said Jack.

"And you," replied Harry.

Uncle Georgie didn't get in just yet. He reached over and turned a switch on the dashboard. Then he began to turn a crank on the side of the automobile. He struggled. The crank looked hard to turn. Finally there was a cough from under the carriage. It gradually turned into a roar. Harry and Jack reached for something to hold onto. The engine was right underneath the front seat, and they could feel it shaking.

Uncle Georgie pulled himself up and took hold of a long L-shaped rod that stuck out of the floor. "This is the steering mechanism," he shouted. They could barely hear him above the engine noise. "It's like the rudder of a boat. When you want to turn right, you turn the rod to the left. And the other way round."

He pressed a pedal on the floor with his foot and pulled a lever on the side of the car. All at once, the automobile lurched forward, knocking Harry and Jack back against the seat. They saw horses rear up, eyes white with fear, as the Oldsmobile started up the road. A man who was trying to control his horse shouted something foul at them and shook his fist.

Uncle Georgie leaned over and spoke, but neither boy could hear him. Jack thought it sounded like, "Someday, everybody–" He finished the sentence in his own mind, but shook his head. If everybody had one of these things, the whole world would be deaf.

Harry didn't pay any attention at all. He was having the time of his life, laughing and holding on with both hands. This was the greatest invention anybody ever came up with!

In a few minutes, they had left the town. Aside from themselves, there was nobody else on the dirt road that led to the lake. "Want to see it go faster?" shouted Uncle Georgie.

"Yes!" replied Harry, and Jack just held on tighter. Uncle Georgie pressed a lever that was attached to the steering rod and they could hear the engine roar. The wind and dust whipped against their faces, making them glad they had the goggles.

"How fast are we going?" Jack asked.

"About twenty miles an hour," replied Uncle Georgie. "I timed it over a one-mile course yesterday."

That was fast, Jack thought, but not as fast as a horse. On the other hand, a horse pulling a wagon couldn't keep up this speed for very long. The noise made the auto seem faster than it was. That and the fact that there was nothing in front of you as it moved along. He put his feet up on top of the little curved dashboard and wondered nervously what would happen if they ran into something.

Fortunately, everything they met on the road got out of the way quickly as soon as it heard them coming. It wasn't more than an hour before they came to Lake Chohobee Village, the little town near Grandpa's house. "I have to buy some fuel," Uncle Georgie told them. He steered the automobile over toward Mr. Pomeroy's general store and pushed a floor pedal that made it stop. Jack and Harry weren't ready, and nearly tumbled over the dashboard.

They had been looking at something else. Right in front of Pomeroy's store stood another automobile. That seemed very strange, since as far as they knew there had never been any automobiles in this town before, and all of a sudden there were two.

"What kind is *that?*" Harry asked.

"It's a Packard," said Uncle Georgie. "I think it's too large to be efficient."

It certainly *was* large, having two full seats, both as big as sofas, and both facing forward. It rode higher than the Oldsmobile, too. The Packard looked like a dray horse next to a pony. Jack wondered whose it was.

A boy walked out of the store, thumbs tucked behind the suspenders that held up his pants. Wearing suspenders was a mistake, because the pants were already too short for him. They ended about an inch above his ankles. He was about sixteen, and he had an expression on his face that Jack didn't like. Sort of the way somebody would look if they felt they owned the town and didn't like other people living in it.

"Hello, Marshall," Uncle Georgie said to the boy. "I need some gasoline."

"I guess we got some," the boy said. He didn't act as if he were in a hurry to get it. "Ain't you gonna ask whose automobile that is?"

"Well, yes, whose is it?"

"It's my daddy's," Marshall said.

Uncle Georgie nodded.

"I guess you Aldriches won't have the only automobile around here now," Marshall said.

Jack nudged Harry, who tried not to laugh. "I guess we won't have the only automobile around here now," said Jack, imitating Marshall's deep voice.

Marshall seemed annoyed. "I guess ours is bigger than yours," he said.

Jack started to reply, but Harry grabbed him and put his hand over Jack's mouth. They fell onto the floor of the car, giggling.

"The Packard is certainly a bigger car," said Uncle Georgie. "Could we get that gasoline now?"

"Bet ours is faster, too," said Marshall.

Jack wrenched free from Harry's grip and stuck his head up. "Bet it's not!" he yelled.

Marshall turned and looked at the two boys as if he hadn't noticed them before. "You think that little Oldsmobile could beat this Packard?"

Uncle Georgie went inside the store. He had decided to find somebody else to give him the gasoline.

Jack and Harry calmed down a little. Marshall was staring at them. They stared back. "I guess you're two more of them Aldriches," Marshall said finally.

"I guess we are," Jack said.

"You're just as stuck-up as the rest of them," Marshall said.

Jack and Harry got out of the Oldsmobile. Harry was nearly as tall as Marshall, and a little wider. Marshall took a step back. "You ever drive that Packard?" Harry asked.

"Well . . . a little ways," Marshall said.

"Why don't we have a race?" Harry said.

"A race?"

"You know. Same as a horse race, only with automobiles." As Harry talked, he was getting more excited. "We could race around the lake."

Marshall thought about it. "There ain't enough room."

"Sure there is," Harry said. "People drive sleighs past each other on that road in the winter."

Marshall was a little uncomfortable now. "Couldn't do it today," he said.

"No, no. Let's do it on the Fourth of July," Harry said. "Everybody could watch it then. You could put up a sign in front of your store here. Get a crowd."

"Have to ask Pa," Marshall mumbled.

Uncle Georgie came out of the store with a can of gasoline. He started to pour it into the Oldsmobile's tank. Jack bent down to look at the engine underneath the car. "I see how it works," he said.

"Yes, the mechanism isn't complicated," said Uncle Georgie.

Jack stood up and looked at Harry. "I know how to make it go faster," he said.

Uncle Georgie smiled. "You boys are so—"

"We're going to have a race," Harry explained to Uncle Georgie.

"Why, I don't know . . ." Uncle Georgie said, blinking.

"Marshall thinks he can beat us," Harry continued.

Uncle Georgie blinked again.

"It will be a good scientific test of the automobiles," Jack told him.

"Well, I guess—"

The boys looked at Marshall. "See you the day after tomorrow," Harry said.

"Unless you're afraid," added Jack.

Marshall set his jaw firmly. "I ain't afraid."

Harry raised his thumbs. "It's a go, then."

On the ride out to Grandpa's house, they convinced Uncle Georgie it was a good idea.

AUTOMOBILE RACE

 BETWEEN

A Packard Automobile
(Owner Sam'l Pomeroy)

An Oldsmobile
(Owner George Aldrich)

July 4
Lake Chohobee Picnic Grounds
Noon

SIX

Don't Forget the Brake

JULY 3, 1902

"I'M AFRAID GEORGIE MAY BE A BAD INFLUENCE on the boys."

That was Great-aunt Zena talking. Peggy was in her own favorite place, the window seat in Grandpa's study. Through the grate, she could hear Grandma and Great-aunt Zena talking in the room downstairs.

Peggy was hiding from Annie, who wanted her to play with her little sister. Nell was cute, but now that she was two and a half and could walk, she followed Peggy everywhere. It got to be a little annoying.

69

Not only that, but now that Jack and Harry were here, all they did was spend time with Uncle Georgie and the automobile. Peggy had hated the machine from the start. It made a terrible racket, it gave off terrible smells, and it bounced her around the one time she rode in it. At least the hot-air balloons had been pretty, floating up in the air like clouds.

So Peggy's ears perked up when she heard Great-aunt Zena's words. If somebody separated the boys from Uncle Georgie, maybe Peggy could have some *fun* again.

Grandma, as usual, was willing to let things be. "I'm not so sure it isn't the other way around," she said.

Aunt Zena's voice sounded surprised. "You don't think this race is advisable?" That was one of her favorite words. Advisable. It meant "good," as far as Peggy could tell.

"Well, Zena," Grandma said. "Boys are always racing one way or another. I've seen them race on foot, on horseback, and in burlap sacks. It doesn't surprise me that they would want to race in automobiles. At least they can't hurt themselves as badly as they might on a horse."

"They would be better off reading an improving book," Aunt Zena said. Peggy almost groaned. An "improving" book meant something that was either very dull or very difficult. Last month, Papa had sent Peggy a new book from Chicago, where he was on tour. It was called *The Wonderful Wizard of Oz*. Unfortunately, Aunt Zena had found Peggy reading it, and inspected the book. She sighed and put it away, telling Peggy it was not an "improving" book.

It was *sort* of improving, Peggy thought. She had improved her detective skills, finding out where Aunt Zena had hidden the book. Then she improved her studying skills by figuring out how to get a stepladder from the kitchen to Aunt Zena's bedroom. She guessed she improved her climbing skills a little bit, too.

"I don't think Laura will approve, either," Aunt Zena was saying now. "It's too bad that she and Richard let the boys come up alone."

"Well, the boys arrived safely," Grandma said. "They're old enough to travel by themselves."

"I don't know," said Aunt Zena. "I think something happened on that train ride. They were arguing about it."

"You worry too much," said Grandma.

Peggy smiled to herself. This time, Aunt Zena was right. The boys had told Peggy about the thief on the train that Harry had almost caught. For some reason, the boys' luggage had been searched, too. But they had sworn Peggy to secrecy, because they didn't want anybody to think it hadn't been safe for them to ride the train alone. "They won't let us do *anything* fun if they think it's dangerous," said Harry.

Peggy had laughed, because Harry was always looking for dangerous things to do.

She stopped daydreaming when she heard her own name mentioned. Annie had come into the room downstairs. "Excuse me, ma'am," she said. "Would you know where Peggy is?"

"She's supposed to be in the classroom composing an essay on the proper use of source notes," said Aunt Zena.

"Oh, no, ma'am. I checked there first," Annie replied. Squealer, Peggy thought. She sighed and slipped out of her secret hiding place. She headed for the back staircase that would get her outside without anybody seeing her.

Keeping well away from the front windows of the house, Peggy went down the path that led to the lake. At the two big pines, she took the right fork toward the space that had been cleared for Grandpa's theater. Grandpa spent almost all his time down there now.

Sure enough, there he was, sitting in a lawn chair with rolls of blueprints on the grass next to him. As he watched, men were climbing ladders and moving around the unfinished building with boards, buckets of plaster, and wheelbarrows filled with stone. The sounds of shouts, hammering, drilling, and clanging echoed throughout the clearing.

Peggy sat on the edge of Grandpa's chair. He looked up and smiled. He seemed much older than he had only a year ago. "When are they going to be finished, Grandpa?" she asked.

"They promised me by the end of the year," he said. "I was hoping we could have a family production."

"That would be fun! You mean cast everybody in the play?"

He nodded. "And then throw open the doors for free and let the townspeople see what the theater is really like."

"What play would you choose?"

"Oh, I have one in mind," he said.

Grandpa enjoyed being mysterious.

"You'd need a play with a lot of children in it," Peggy said.

"Yes, I know," said Grandpa.

"Would you be in it too?"

"I don't think so," he said. "I want to be the director. I'm too old to act anymore."

"Oh, no, you're not." Peggy gave him a hug. "You do it all the time."

He smiled and took out his watch. The case popped open and the little song played. "Oh, my!" he said with a look of alarm.

"What's the matter?"

"Someone is supposed to be in the classroom, and she's not there."

"Oh, Grandpa." She knew he didn't really care. "It's not fair. Jack and Harry are already out of school for the whole summer. I so looked forward to them being here, and now they're spending the whole day working on that . . . machine."

Just then, they heard the engine of the Oldsmobile start. It was louder than it had been earlier.

"Why did you buy Uncle Georgie the automobile anyway?" she asked. "It's noisy and it smells terrible."

"Oh, well, I wanted to get him away from the hot-air balloons," Grandpa said. "Everyone was afraid he was going to start a serious fire."

Peggy nodded. She remembered that Uncle Georgie had wanted her to row out onto the lake and set fire to the boat. Only Harry would have been crazy enough to do that, and fortunately he wasn't there.

"I thought he couldn't do much harm with the automobile," said Grandpa thoughtfully. "I made him promise to keep it out of the house."

"But then you had to keep him from storing it in the barn, too," Peggy pointed out.

Grandpa wagged his eyebrows. "It would have been too cruel to the horses. Speaking of horses—" He glanced at her. "Michael tells me you've become an excellent rider."

"Last week, he let me take Shakespeare for a canter. Of course, it was only inside the paddock."

"Why don't we go down to the barn and you can show me how good you are?" he said.

Peggy was thrilled. Grandpa struggled to his feet, using the cane he carried everywhere now. Once he started walking though, he didn't really seem to need it.

Before they reached the barn, the Oldsmobile darted out from the shed that had been built to hold it. Harry was holding onto the tiller, Jack was next to him shouting something they couldn't hear, and Uncle Georgie was running along behind. Both Harry and Jack were wearing goggles and Peggy wondered how they could see clearly.

Grandpa took Peggy by the arm and stepped quickly behind a large pine tree. It was a wise move, because Harry didn't seem to have figured out how to stop the machine. He kept turning the tiller, causing it to zigzag back and forth. As he passed near their tree, they could hear him shouting, "Whoa! Whoa!"

But that only worked with horses. Finally, Harry managed to turn the auto in a complete circle and headed it back toward the shed. Uncle Georgie, who'd been following, was now standing right in the path of the Oldsmobile. "Watch out!" Peggy shouted, but instead of getting out of the way, he turned and ran.

Uncle Georgie was faster than Peggy expected. He had long legs, and probably would have gotten away from the Oldsmobile. Except that he ran back inside the shed. The automobile, almost like a horse returning to the barn, followed him right back in. Just before it disappeared, Peggy saw Jack dive onto the floor of the machine.

A tremendous crash and the sound of splintering wood followed. Then everything was quiet. Peggy didn't realize how annoying the noise of the engine was until it stopped. But that meant—she ran toward the shed, and Grandpa hobbled right along behind.

Her eyes widened when she saw what was inside. It took her a second to figure out what had happened. Uncle Georgie was hanging from a rope that was attached to a beam overhead. He must have jumped up there, letting the automobile pass underneath him until it ran into the back wall of the shed and finally stopped.

Harry was still in the front seat. He turned around with a big happy smile on his face and said to nobody in particular, "Wasn't that *great?*"

Just then, Jack's head popped up from the floor and he yelled, "The brake is down there! You have to step on it to stop! I told you!"

Harry's face fell, but only a little. "I know, Jack. I just forgot. I kept thinking I had to pull on the reins."

"There aren't any *reins!* It's an automobile!"

"They should have reins on it. That way it'd be easier to control."

Uncle Georgie dropped from the rope. "The wheels!" he cried. "Are they damaged?"

They went around to the front of the car. Both of the wheels had gone through the back wall of the shed. They were strong, though, and except for one or two broken spokes there didn't seem to be much damage. "We can fix that by tomorrow," Jack said.

Grandpa had finally caught up and heard what Jack had said. "You rascals aren't going anywhere tomorrow," he sputtered. "You can stay here and shoot off fireworks and have a safe Independence Day." He turned to Uncle Georgie. "You, too!"

The boys began to protest, and so did Uncle Georgie. "It's perfectly safe," he said. "You can see for yourself that the automobile can't tip over, and it's made of wood, steel, and rubber. You could almost crash it into a tree without hurting yourself."

Grandpa snorted. "Weren't you running for your life just a minute ago?"

"Well, there won't be any people in front of us during the race, Grandpa," said Jack. "And by tomorrow, Harry will know how to steer." He muttered, "and use the brake," in a voice that Grandpa didn't hear.

But Peggy did. "Why isn't Uncle Georgie going to drive the car?" she asked.

"Jack showed me how the car could be made to go faster," said Uncle Georgie. "In return, I agreed that they could take the controls in the race."

"How can it go faster?" Peggy asked Jack.

"Crawl under the car and I'll show you," he replied.

She looked at the grease and oil that had soaked into the floor of the shed. Jack had some of it on his clothes and face. "Forget that!" she said.

Grandpa shook his cane at the boys. "Well, when your father and mother arrive, they may have something else to say about this." He took Peggy's hand and said, "Come along. Let's see how you do on a horse."

She followed along. As they left the shed, Grandpa said, "You see? Now *there* is an example of something that didn't need to be invented."

"I'd much rather ride a horse," Peggy agreed.

"And you know what?" said Grandpa. "You can ride Shakespeare tomorrow."

"Tomorrow?" she asked.

"Look up at the sky," he told her.

She did. "It's gray and cloudy."

"What direction is the wind coming from?"

Peggy saw the clouds moving and thought for a second. "From the southeast?"

"That's right," Grandpa said. He stopped and pointed in that direction. "The ocean is that way. And that means it's going to rain. Rain hard."

She nodded. "But—" She didn't understand.

He turned to her and said, "It means that Shakespeare will be able to beat either one of those noisy what-you-may-call-its."

"The automobiles?" Peggy giggled at what Uncle Georgie would say if that were true.

SEVEN

Three at the Starting Line

JUST AS GRANDPA HAD SAID, IT STARTED TO RAIN. Uncle Richard and Aunt Laura arrived ten minutes after it began. Michael had gone to the station to pick them up in a horse-drawn carriage, so they didn't know about the Oldsmobile yet.

"An automobile?" said Aunt Laura when Great-aunt Zena told them. "How like Georgie to have one of those disgusting things."

Great-aunt Zena told them more.

"Well, if he's going to race with it," said Aunt Laura, "at least it will be going away from us as fast as possible." She laughed at her own joke.

81

And then Great-aunt Zena told them the worst part.

Aunt Laura was speechless. For a second. "Harry? And Jack?" she said. "In an automobile? *Racing?*"

"It's really not going to be a race," Jack explained quickly. "It's more like a test of the automobiles."

"Just like in school," Harry added.

Everybody looked at him. He blushed. "Well, anyway," he said. "I can already ride a horse and drive a carriage. An automobile is lots easier."

"Harry drove it all around today," Jack said. "He's an expert."

"In the future—" Uncle Georgie began, but everybody turned and told him to hush.

Aunt Laura threw up her hands. She looked at her husband. "Richard," she said. "I leave this up to you. Do you want your sons to risk their safety in some wild escapade merely for . . . for thrills?"

Peggy admired the way Aunt Laura said *thrills*. She made it sound like it had at least three syllables and was the worst thing you could imagine.

So everybody knew what Uncle Richard was going to say.

Except he didn't.

"I think it sounds like a lot of fun," he said with a big smile, the same smile that playgoers loved all over the country.

"Hooray!" Harry and Jack yelled. They were so excited they ran out of the room. Of course, Peggy realized, maybe they didn't want to wait for their mother to change their father's mind.

⋇≈◉◡≈⋇

That night it rained and rained. Peggy lay in bed listening to the sound of it long after the lamps were turned out. The windows were open because it was a warm night, and the sound of the rain drowned out everything else.

Jack and Harry, snug under fresh sheets in their own beds, slept soundly. The sound of rain was soothing, and they were dreaming about the wonderful day that tomorrow would be.

The rain stopped finally, just before dawn. When the sun peeped above the horizon, its rays glimmered off the still, shining surfaces of a million puddles. As Bridget opened the back door of the kitchen to bring in firewood, she looked around and said, "Oh, my! Muddy!"

Half an hour later, Michael the groom went to check on the horses. He led Shakespeare out of his stall. Just as Grandpa had told him to do the day before, Michael began to put mud cleats on the big stallion.

One by one, everybody in the big house began to wake up. The boys were happy to see that it looked like a bright, sunny day. They threw on their clothes and clattered down the stairs, waking anybody who might still have been asleep. "Let's eat and get the car started!" said Harry.

"No, the race won't start till noon," Jack said. "We don't want to overheat the Oldsmobile by running it too much beforehand."

Harry didn't reply. Secretly he felt that he needed a little more practice driving, but he didn't want Jack to mention that to Uncle Georgie. By the time Harry had downed half a dozen of Bridget's flapjacks, he forgot about it himself.

Peggy came downstairs and said, "Hey, you two! Save some for me!" She was wearing a long riding dress.

Jack noticed. "Where are you going?" he asked.

"I thought I would ride along in the race," she said casually.

Jack stared at her. "You can't do that," he said.

"Why not?" she asked, spreading strawberry jam on a piece of toast.

"Well—it's an *automobile* race, that's why."

She tossed her long red hair back. Harry and Jack looked at each other. They had seen her do that before, and knew what it meant. She was going to do what she wanted.

"Your horse will be scared of the noise, Peg," Jack pointed out. "You could get thrown."

"Michael says Shakespeare is used to the Oldsmobile because he's heard Uncle Georgie driving it," she replied.

"Shakespeare?" Harry asked. "Who says you can ride Shakespeare?"

"Grandpa," she said, licking jam off her fingers.

"He wouldn't let *us* ride Shakespeare last summer," said Harry.

"You didn't have Michael to teach you, like I did," Peggy said.

"We can't stop to help you if you get thrown," Jack warned.

Shakespeare

"Not even if you're trampled," added Harry.

"I won't expect you to," she said.

After breakfast, Peggy went to the stables. Michael gave her a carrot to feed Shakespeare, and she brushed the big stallion's coat. Shakespeare turned his head to look at her.

"He's ready for a nice ride," said Michael. "He likes to run in the mud. It cools his feet. But you should let the automobiles go on ahead."

"I can't do that," Peggy said. "I want to beat them."

"Oh, sure you do," said Michael. "And you will. But if you start out in front, Shakespeare will just run to get away from them. He'll tire himself."

"But sometime I've got to pass the others," she said.

"The race will go all around the lake, isn't that right?" Michael asked.

"Yes. It starts and ends at the picnic grounds." He smiled. "You'll pass the automobiles as if they were standing still."

⋅⊱⊰⋅

The nice weather brought a big crowd to the picnic grounds at the shore of the lake. Of course, there were seventeen people from the Aldrich family alone. Bridget packed two big hampers of fried chicken, cucumber sandwiches, apples, oranges, pickles, potato salad, and more. She sent the ice-cream bucket along, too, filled with fresh cream and dry ice. Everybody took a turn at winding the crank around and around, waiting for the cream to become ice cream. Even the youngest children, Freddy and Nell, happily turned the crank once or twice, thinking it was part of a game.

A lot of townspeople arrived with their own picnic baskets. Everybody had seen the poster announcing the race, and there was a buzz of excitement in the air. The Pomeroys arrived in their big Packard automobile, polished and shining. People gathered around it, reaching out to touch it, as if it were some kind of dangerous animal. Nobody seemed to notice that a lot of mud had already stuck to its thick rubber tires.

When Jack and Harry drove into the picnic grounds, the crowd moved in their direction. Arguments started to break out. Which automobile looked better? Some said the large, powerful-looking Packard with its luxurious leather seats. Others liked the sporty lines of the Oldsmobile.

And of course, people also disagreed about which one would prove faster. "I'll bet a dollar on the Packard!" announced one man, and somebody else called, "I'll take it."

That started another buzz of activity. Hands were shaken, bets were made, and people backed their choices.

Then Grandpa Aldrich stood up in his wagon and waved his cane. "I have another bet!" he called out. People turned, because his deep stage voice was almost as strong as ever. Seeing that he had the crowd's attention, Grandpa spoke even louder. "I'll bet anyone up to a hundred dollars that my granddaughter finishes the race before either of these smoke-buggies."

The crowd buzzed. People weren't quite sure what Grandpa was talking about. Then Michael helped Peggy get up onto Shakespeare's back. A few people started to laugh when they saw her. "She's just a girl!" somebody said. Another voice cried out, "A horse can't beat an automobile over that distance!"

Some of the men looked at each other and then moved forward to place bets with Grandpa. If the old man wanted to throw away his money, why, they'd be pleased to take some. Mr. Pomeroy jumped down from the front seat of the Packard and stepped up to Grandpa's wagon. He offered a bet of ten dollars that his automobile would finish ahead of the horse. Grandpa smiled and accepted, writing it down in a little notebook.

Mr. Benjamin, the mayor of the town, accepted the job of starting the race. He had brought along a pistol loaded with blanks. "Is everybody aware of the length of the race?" he asked. "Once around the lake, finishing back at this line." He drew a line on the ground with a stick, and the two cars moved right up to it. Harry, Jack, and Marshall Pomeroy all shifted their goggles into place and adjusted their caps.

"Ah . . . is the horse ready too?" Mr. Benjamin asked. Peggy, seated on Shakespeare, was still off to one side, with Michael holding its bridle. "She's giving them a head start," Michael explained.

Mr. Benjamin shook his head in disbelief. "Whatever you like," he said.

"All ready now!" he shouted. "Keep out of the way!"

People lined up on either side of the road, eager to see how fast the automobiles would start. Others, unfortunately, decided to stand in back of the starting line. They regretted it. When Mr. Benjamin shot off his pistol to start the race, both drivers threw their automobiles into gear.

Immediately, outraged shouts and screams came from the spectators in back. The wheels of the automobiles spun wildly, throwing thick globs of mud behind them. Peggy had to put her hand over her mouth as she watched the crowd scatter and try to get out of the way.

The people alongside the road didn't fare much better. Finally the tires of the Oldsmobile caught hold and Harry and Jack shot forward. But the automobile had no mud guards, and it sprayed a filthy, thick stream of water onto everybody on its side of the road.

Those on the other side, seeing this, broke into shouts of laughter. Almost immediately, the Packard passed by and left them as mud-spattered and angry as the other side, which now had their turn to laugh.

Michael let go of Shakespeare's bridle, and gave him a little pat. "Now it's your turn," he said to Peggy. She laughed as she kicked Shakespeare's sides. When she galloped after the automobiles, she was the only person in sight who wasn't dripping with mud.

EIGHT

Who's in Front?

JULY 4, 1902

HARRY KNEW HE'D NEVER FORGET THE WAY HE FELT now, and forever after would want to feel that way again. He was thrilled to be at the tiller of an automobile that must be traveling at least thirty miles an hour. He turned his head for a moment and saw that the Packard was still far behind. That only made him want to go faster, and he pulled the throttle back as far as it would go.

Of course, he was terrified, too. The muddy road was much more slippery than he expected. Driving on it was nothing like driving around the yard at Grandpa's house. He knew that at any minute he might lose all control of the automobile.

It was going to take every bit of nerve and skill he had to keep it on the road.

That was the most thrilling thing of all.

"You don't have to go so *fast!*" That was Jack, shouting at him just because the Packard wasn't close. Jack didn't understand how it felt to *want* to go fast, faster than anybody else could. Just *because* it was so frightening.

Jack realized he should have let Harry drive the Oldsmobile all by himself. He didn't know why he wanted to come along. Because, as usual, Harry was trying to be a hero by doing something that was impossibly stupid and dangerous.

It was his own fault, Jack realized. He had figured out how to adjust the engine to make the automobile go faster. He had gotten Uncle Georgie to agree to let Harry drive. And of course, he wanted to go along to see if everything worked right.

No, that wasn't all of it. He came along because Harry did things Jack wouldn't have dared to do alone.

Jack looked back. The Packard seemed to be gaining on them. Because it was so heavy, it took a while for it to get up to full speed. He turned to face the front again. They were coming to a curve, and Harry would have to slow down.

But instead Harry turned the tiller long before they reached the curve. The front wheels of the car started to skid. Jack held onto the dashboard with all his strength. He wondered whether he would be better off being thrown clear of the car or staying in it till it crashed.

Amazingly, the car seemed to be moving sideways toward the curve. Then, at the last minute, the wheels seemed to catch hold of something dry under the mud. The Oldsmobile shot around the curve like the last boy in a crack-the-whip game. Jack realized that his fingers were numb from holding on so tightly.

Harry didn't know why he'd decided to turn the tiller so far ahead of the curve. He was glad it worked, though. He felt himself grinning and looked over at Jack. He'd hear from Jack later about the way they took the turn. Jack would have figured out some reason why it worked. Then he'd write it down so he wouldn't forget. Harry wouldn't need to write it down. He knew he'd never forget how to do it again.

When he looked up ahead though, he wasn't so happy. The road was straight for a long way here. They wouldn't reach another turn till the very top of the lake. If the Packard caught them on this straight stretch, it could go right past. Except that there didn't seem to be enough room for both cars side by side. *That* was going to cause some trouble, Harry knew. He grinned again.

Every time Jack looked back, the Packard was a little closer to them. He would certainly like to take a look at its engine sometime. But even if the

Packard did catch up, there wasn't enough room here for it to pass. So he wasn't worried a bit.

Just then, Harry took the Oldsmobile at full speed through a puddle of water. Jack felt a bump, as if the car had struck something hard. At the same time, the Oldsmobile slowed down.

"Keep going!" Jack yelled. "He's gaining on us!"

"Something's wrong!" Harry shouted back.

The water might have gotten into the engine, Jack realized. He turned his head and saw the Packard go through the same puddle, shooting up an enormous spray of water. Its front wheels wobbled, but then it came forward as fast as before.

"He's going to catch us!" Jack told Harry.

Harry just shook his head, trying to squeeze every bit of speed out of the Oldsmobile.

Jack couldn't look anywhere but behind them as the Packard edged closer. Pretty soon its radiator was only a few feet in back of them. He could see Marshall Pomeroy turning the wheels back and forth, trying to find space to get by.

Finally Marshall managed to creep up next to them on the lake side of the road. The noise of both engines roaring side by side was deafening. Jack looked ahead of them. They were approaching the sharp curve at the top of the lake. It would be impossible for them both to get around it at once.

Marshall Pomeroy saw it, too. As soon as the front of his car was a few feet in front of the Oldsmobile, he began to edge over toward them.

"What's he doing?" Jack called out. "Hey! Pomeroy! Stay away!"

Harry had to turn the tiller to keep from hitting the Packard. "He's trying to run us off the road!" he shouted at Jack.

Jack looked over his side of the car. There was a ditch there, filled with water, and the Oldsmobile's front wheels were dangerously close to it.

"Slow down!" he told Harry. "Let him pass us!"

Harry turned toward Jack. Jack couldn't see his eyes through the goggles but he suddenly knew what Harry was thinking.

Before Jack could stop him, Harry turned the tiller in the other direction. The front of the Oldsmobile headed straight for the side of the Packard.

Bang! Their front left wheel hit the other car and scraped along it with a terrible sound of shrieking metal. Jack could see Marshall Pomeroy struggle to keep the Packard under control.

Marshall must have hit his brake pedal, because the Packard suddenly fell back. Jack turned and saw that it was skidding crazily on the muddy road. Then he felt the Oldsmobile slow down, too.

Even Harry realized that it was crazy to take the hairpin turn at full speed. But maybe it was too late. As they started into the turn, Jack felt the back wheels sliding to the right. At the same time, Harry was struggling to keep the front wheels aimed straight ahead. The Oldsmobile started to spin.

⋯≡◎⊂≡⋯

Peggy was watching the whole thing. Riding high up on Shakespeare, she had a better view of the race than anyone. She was certainly glad that Michael had told her to stay behind the two automobiles. The way the boys were driving, they would have frightened Shakespeare.

Michael had promised her she'd pass the automobiles before the race was over. Now, as she came nearer, it looked as if she would get the chance. Marshall Pomeroy's Packard was stuck in the mud. He was racing his engine as fast as he could. It sounded like it was full of angry bees, only louder. The front wheel on the right side of the car spun so quickly that it started to smoke. But the wheels on the left side wouldn't budge at all.

Marshall Pomeroy turned as Peggy rode up. He looked angry. His face was red and sweaty. "Your brother is crazy!" he said.

"He's not my brother. He's my cousin," she replied, but Marshall didn't hear her.

"He cheated!" Marshall went on. "He pushed me right off the road."

Peggy brought Shakespeare to a stop. He bobbed his head, because he was enjoying the ride. "I saw the whole thing," Peggy told Marshall. "You tried to run them into the ditch over there."

"I needed room to pass," he protested.

"You could have waited," she said. "The road is wider on the other side of the lake."

Marshall got out and tried to push the car. All that did was get his shoes muddy. "I won't forget this!" he said as Peggy flicked the reins and signaled Shakespeare it was time to run some more.

"I guess you won't," she murmured, looking ahead of her. She couldn't see what had happened to the Oldsmobile. Marshall was still shouting as Peggy rode off, but she wasn't listening any longer.

Jack was trying to get Harry to slow down. "I can't even see the Packard anymore," he said. "I think he's broken down."

They had had a pretty close call themselves, at the top of the lake. The Oldsmobile had spun completely around in a 180-degree turn. Jack was afraid that the wheels had bent. And then Harry started off in the wrong direction. After he realized that the lake had moved to the opposite side of the car, he had to turn around. And now he was trying to make up for lost time.

"Pomeroy might have passed us when we were turning around," Harry shouted back.

"That's impossible!" Jack yelled. He looked toward the rear, and this time he saw something. He strained to look, because he could hardly believe his eyes.

"Peggy's behind us," he told Harry.

Harry turned to look for himself. "Pomeroy *must* be ahead of us," he said. "She could never have passed him."

Jack tried to think. He knew Pomeroy couldn't have gone past them without being seen. "It doesn't matter," he said. "Peggy won't catch us."

But Harry drove as if a fiend in a flaming chariot were breathing down their necks. All Jack could do was hold on and hope that they didn't go spinning into the lake. Harry was hardly slowing down for the turns now. He seemed to have figured out a way to go into them and come out even faster.

Jack turned his head and saw that Peggy was still in sight. No matter how fast Harry drove, she seemed to keep up.

He wiped his goggles. The mud was sloppier on this side of the lake, and they needed cleaning more often. The car roared over the crest of a hill. At the bottom was a little bridge where a stream flowed into the lake.

Jack felt as if his heart had stopped. The stream had overflowed its banks during the rainstorm. Now, at the bottom of the hill, there was a huge, wet pool of mud. Harry didn't care. He pulled the throttle all the way out. They sped down the hill faster than they had been going the whole race.

"Stop!" Jack shouted, but Harry paid no attention. Jack fell onto the floor and tried to reach the brake again. It was too late. As the Oldsmobile roared into the mud, he was thrown forward against the dashboard. The car came to a jolting halt, and as Jack looked up, Harry disappeared.

⊶══◉═══⊷

Peggy wanted to laugh when she saw what happened, but then she realized that Harry might have been hurt. When the Oldsmobile stopped so suddenly, he was thrown right over the top of the dashboard. He landed face-first in the mud, skidding along until he came to a stop.

As Peggy urged Shakespeare to go faster, she saw Harry slowly roll over. He looked like a chocolate candy man. Then he pulled up his goggles, and he looked like a candy man wearing a white blindfold. Harry's eyes shone, and Peggy knew he was all right.

"Hey, Peggy," he called as she rode up. "Did you see that?"

"Yes, I was so worried," she said.

"Wasn't that *great?*"

"Are you crazy?" That was Jack, sitting in the car and checking to see if he had any broken arms or legs. "You could have been killed! Even worse, *I* could have been killed!"

Harry paid no attention. Jack was always complaining. "Listen, Peggy," he said. "Have you got a rope?"

"No," she said. "Why?"

"I think we're going to need a rope to get the car out of this mud. If we tied a rope to it, Shakespeare could pull us out."

"That's a good idea, Harry," she said. "I'll come back with a rope." She looked at Jack. "You're not hurt, either?"

He shook his head.

"Then I'll see you both later," she said.

"Wait!" Harry said. "Is Pomeroy behind us?"

"Oh, yes," she told him. "He's stuck in the mud farther back."

Harry smiled. After Peggy had ridden off, he said, "You know, if she comes back soon, we could still win the race."

Jack stared at him. "Are you sure you didn't land on your head?"

"I *did* land on my head," Harry said.

"Look, Harry," said Jack. "Peggy is going to win the race."

Harry thought about it a second and nodded. "Sure," he said, "but we could still win the *automobile* race."

September 14, 1902

Dear Jack,

I suppose you and Harry are back at school now. You are so lucky to spend at least the summers with your parents. Well, of course Mama is here and Papa comes pretty often, but what I miss is being able to go to the theater every night. Sometimes I was even in some of the plays when they needed an extra juvenile.

Uncle Georgie was able to repair the Oldsmobile. He says it runs better than ever, so you and Harry are forgiven. Grandpa still teases Uncle Georgie about me winning the race on a horse. But Uncle

Georgie says the same thing you did—if the weather hadn't been rainy, I wouldn't have had a chance.

Grandpa gave me five dollars out of the money he won. I used some of it to buy more film for my camera. I have some really nice shots of the Fourth of July celebration. Don't tell Harry, but I got one of him before he washed off all the mud.

You'd be surprised to see how much of Grandpa's theater has been built. I think they will finish it by New Year's. He still wants to put on a play that everybody in the family can appear in. He won't tell us what the play is though. And now he says there will be some other surprises as well. I'll let you know if I learn anything more.

I almost forgot to tell you. Mr. Pomeroy has opened a moving picture theater next to his general store. I guess you've seen moving pictures in New York. They're like the magic lantern slide shows, except that the pictures seem to move. Mama and I each paid a nickel to see them one afternoon. That's why they call it a Nickelodeon—it costs a nickel to get in. They really do move.

Of course, Uncle Georgie says the moving pictures are

the wave of the future. And
that makes Grandpa angry.
He won't even go into town to
see them. He says it's just a
novelty.

 It is, I suppose. If you
could tell a story with them,
maybe they would become popular. But it's nothing like a
stage play. They don't seem
real. Grandpa's right about
that.

 Write back and tell me
what's going on at school.

Your cousin,
Peggy

October 1, 1902

Dear Peggy,

   Harry wants me to ask you to
find out if there are going to be any
pirates in Grandpa's play. Not too
much is happening at school. The
science teacher showed us that you can
put a little blob of potassium in water
and it will burn with a purple flame.
It's quite impressive. However, the
potassium is stored in a locked cabinet
in the science lab. Too bad, because
I would enjoy trying it myself. I have
some ideas for using it.

                              Your cousin,
                              Jack

October 16, 1902

Dear Jack,

Grandpa says he will put some pirates in the play. I found out that he is writing it himself. I showed him your letter and it gave him an idea. He says he will get you some potassium! It's for the play, though. He wants to have a fire on stage. Sometime in December he will send you and Harry the parts he wants you to memorize. I must admit I'm getting a little excited about it.

Your cousin,
Peggy

FREE!!

THE WORLD PREMIER PERFORMANCE

OF THE PIRATES' MISTAKE

A New Play
by Lionel Aldrich
December 31, 1902

at the Aldrich Theater
Lake Chohobee Road

FREE ADMISSION

NINE

Two Visitors

DECEMBER 30, 1902

PEGGY HAD NEVER SEEN GRANDPA SO ANGRY. Just as the workers were putting the finishing touches on the theater, who should arrive but Mr. Pomeroy. He said he was the town fire marshal and it was his duty to inspect the theater.

Grandpa said they had no time. They were going to start rehearsing the play. The scenery had just arrived. It had to be unpacked and set up. The lights had to be tested. There were a million things to do.

Peggy didn't see how they were going to rehearse when half the cast still hadn't arrived yet. Papa and Uncle Richard and Aunt Laura and the boys were still in New York. She thought Grandpa should just let Mr. Pomeroy inspect and get that over with.

But the two of them had been feuding ever since the Fourth of July. Mr. Pomeroy had tried not to pay Grandpa when he lost the bet. He claimed that Jack and Harry had cheated. They had run Marshall off the road with their car, and that was the reason Peggy won the race. Grandpa had said only a knave would refuse to pay his wagers. Finally, Mr. Pomeroy did, but he put in a few choice words of his own for free. Not long afterward, he opened his nickelodeon. Peggy thought it was to take business away from Grandpa's theater. Now here he was again.

Peggy sent Polly and Molly up to the house to tell their mother what was happening. Pretty soon Grandma and Aunt Maud and Mama arrived and tried to smooth things over. Grandma kept taking Grandpa by the arm, telling him to calm down.

He'd been working for over a year on the theater, and stayed up late writing the play, too. Peggy had heard Aunt Maud tell Mama he was pushing himself too hard. But nobody could persuade him to slow down.

Right now, though, Grandma had pulled him away from Mr. Pomeroy. "We have plenty of time to rehearse, Lionel," Grandma said. "Let this man look at the theater, and he'll leave."

"He has no right," Grandpa protested. But it looked like the argument was over.

Just at that moment, however, Uncle Georgie showed up carrying a small stove. That was what it looked like, anyway. What it really was, Peggy knew, was the machine that heated air for the hot-air balloons. Grandpa was going to use a balloon in the play.

"Where are you going with that?" Mr. Pomeroy asked sharply.

Uncle Georgie looked puzzled. "In there," he said, pointing to the door that led to the stage.

Mr. Pomeroy's eyes narrowed and his nose wrinkled as if he smelled trouble. "What's it for?"

"Why, it's—" Georgie began, but Grandpa interrupted him.

"It's a prop!" Grandpa announced. "We're putting it on the stage."

Mr. Pomeroy sniffed the air. "It smells like you've been using it."

"Why, yes," said Uncle Georgie.

"To burn something?"

"No," said Grandpa at the same time that Georgie said, "Yes."

"That is," Grandpa explained, "we did use it for burning, but we're not going to on stage."

Uncle Georgie looked surprised. "I thought we were going to . . . "

"No," Grandpa said, shaking his head. "Take the stove back. I've changed my mind. I've decided not to use it."

"There's no other way to get a balloon into the air," Georgie protested.

"Balloon?" said Mr. Pomeroy.

"We don't need the balloon now," said Grandpa.

"How about children? I heard you are going to use children in the play," said Mr. Pomeroy.

"Oh?" Grandpa said. "I thought you were the fire inspector. Are you the children inspector, too?"

Grandma stepped between them. She spoke quietly to Mr. Pomeroy. "We wanted this to be a play that families could bring their children to. It will be suitable for children, and yes, some of our grandchildren will be in it."

Mr. Pomeroy frowned. "I'll have to see if there's a law against that."

"Go right ahead," said Grandpa smugly. Peggy had a feeling he had already looked up the law.

Mr. Pomeroy inspected the building, with Grandpa and everybody else following right behind. He didn't seem to find anything wrong. Peggy knew he would have been sure to mention it if he had. "I see you're using electric lighting," he said.

"Yes," Grandpa replied. "Everything is going to be completely modern."

When Mr. Pomeroy left, Peggy asked Grandpa, "I remember when you didn't like electric lights, Grandpa."

"I still don't," he told her. "But some people are trying to pass a law against using gas lighting in theaters. They think it's more likely to cause fires. So I decided to avoid trouble. By the way," he added, with a sharp look, "if anyone asks, you have been going to school with a tutor."

"Well, I have," she said. "Only the tutor was Great-aunt Zena."

"You don't have to mention her name," he said. "And also make sure that you tell them you only work in the theater four hours a day."

"That's true, too," she said.

"Fine. Now where did Georgie go? I want him to bring the heater back in here again."

"Are we still going to use the balloon on stage?" she asked.

"Yes, it will be a great scene," he said. "You'll have to learn how to bring it down. Shouldn't be any trouble, if Georgie can do it. Oh, and Freddy and Nell will be up there with you. Don't tell anyone how old they are."

Peggy smiled. "You can see that they're almost babies."

"Well, if they're up in the balloon, people might think they're midgets."

She laughed. "Nobody is going to believe they're midgets, Grandpa."

He nodded. "We'll just have to keep that busybody Pomeroy out of the theater somehow."

⋆⟞⊜⟝⋆

Harry and Jack arrived just before dinnertime. Michael and Peggy went to the station to meet them in a horse and carriage. Grandpa had made Uncle Georgie lock the Oldsmobile in its storage shed. He told Uncle Georgie that he didn't want anything to distract the boys until the play was over.

The boys were excited anyway. Grandpa had done more than put pirates in the play. He had cast both the boys as pirates. Harry had practiced fencing at school, hoping that his role would include a sword fight. And then Grandpa had promised that Jack could devise some stage effects with potassium.

But now that Mr. Pomeroy had been snooping around, Grandpa wasn't so sure. "It's perfectly safe," Jack insisted. They were doing a walk-through rehearsal at the theater after dinner. The stage smelled of fresh paint and sawdust, reminding Peggy of the wonderful times she'd had with Mama and Papa on the road.

"This man Pomeroy will use any excuse to shut the theater down," Grandpa told Jack. "He has a grudge against us for some reason. I think he'd make a fuss even if we only shot off fireworks."

"Let me have some of the potassium and I'll show you," Jack said.

"Not now, not now," Grandpa told him. "Let's think about how it can be used. I want a scene where the audience can see ships burning in the background." He showed them the miniature ships that would float in a trough at the back of the stage.

Jack's eyes glittered. "We can put the potassium right in the water, and it will make those ships go up in flames. Purple flames. It will be wonderful."

Just then Harry let out a whoop. He had found the ropes that the pirates would use to swing from their ship onto another ship. He wasted no time in trying one out, soaring over the stage from one side to the other. He let go at just the right moment and landed on the deck of the other ship.

"Your father couldn't have done it better," Grandpa said.

"Really?" Harry's face lit up as if Santa Claus had given him a present.

"Now I want to see how you are at a sword fight." Grandpa brought a pair of prop swords out of a chest and handed one to Harry.

"Who am I going to fight?" Harry asked.

"You can practice with me," Grandpa said. "But in the play, you will fight your father."

Harry's eyes widened. "Oh, I don't want to fight him."

"And you'll have to lose, too," added Grandpa. "Because you know, he always plays the hero."

Harry's face had gone through a lot of changes in a few seconds, Peggy thought. Now he looked as if he had opened his present and it were a lump of coal. But he took the sword from Grandpa anyway.

Peggy and Jack watched them practice. "Harry's very good," Peggy said.

"He's been working at it," Jack replied. "What is your role in the play?"

"I'm one of the children kidnapped by the pirates," she said. "But we escape in a balloon. Provided Mr. Pomeroy doesn't find out."

"You have all the fun," he said.

"Well, we aren't going very far," she told him. "Just up in the air and out of sight behind the rafters. Then, when the scenery is changed, we'll come back down again."

"You don't know where Grandpa keeps the potassium, do you?" he asked. "It would be in a jar of yellow liquid."

She did know, but just said, "Jack, you'd use it all up before the play begins."

Peggy's mother and Aunt Maud came down from the house then, bringing Polly and Molly with them. They told Grandpa he had to explain the twins' parts to them now, because it would soon be their bedtime.

The twins would be lost on the island that was the pirates' headquarters. Grandpa had planned something that was sure to draw a laugh. Polly would walk off the right side of the stage at the same time that Molly entered at stage left. Because the audience wouldn't know there were two of them, it would look like a magic trick.

The twins just had to get the timing right, so that the two of them would never be seen at the same time. But they caught on quickly. "They're Aldriches, all right," Grandpa said proudly.

"Yes, and here are the rest of us," came a voice from the back of the theater. It was Uncle Richard. He and Aunt Laura and Uncle Nick marched down the aisle, still dressed in their winter over-coats. Peggy saw that Papa was with them, too, and another man. She shaded her eyes to see who he was.

Grandpa didn't notice the man at first. "We weren't expecting you until tomorrow," he called to Richard from the stage.

"We couldn't turn down the chance to travel in our own railroad car," Uncle Richard said.

By now Peggy was able to see the man clearly. She could hardly believe it. But there was no mistaking the big-toothed smile, bushy mustache, and the thick glasses balanced on his nose.

"Your own car?" Grandpa was puzzled.

And then another voice, high-pitched, came out of the back of the theater. "Lionel, don't you know I get a railroad car with my new job?"

It was Theodore Roosevelt, president of the United States.

TEN

An Obstacle Hike

"HOW DO YOU KNOW THE PRESIDENT, GRANDPA?" Peggy asked.

"Oh, from long ago, when he was police commissioner of New York City," Grandpa said. "We used to meet for dinner at Delmonico's after the theaters closed. Who would have thought then—" He trailed off.

But the president laughed and finished the sentence. "Who would have thought that a cowboy like me would turn out to be president." He clasped Grandpa's hand. "Well, Lionel, it was as big a surprise to me as it was to you."

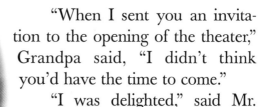

President Roosevelt

"When I sent you an invitation to the opening of the theater," Grandpa said, "I didn't think you'd have the time to come."

"I was delighted," said Mr. Roosevelt. "I sent your son Dick a telegram to let him know I'd be coming through New York. We picked up him and Laura at Grand Central Station. It was a good opportunity for the children to get out of Washington. It's an unhealthy town, in my view."

The president had brought along his own children—Teddy Jr., Kermit, Ethel, Archie, and Quentin. They were practically the same ages as Harry, Jack, and Peggy. And they were pretty much as lively and full of fun as the Aldriches, too. They all wanted to be in the play, and Grandma hunted up a few more costumes so they could be pirates or kidnapped children.

The president was backstage, too, poking into everything and asking questions. As soon as he found out about the hot-air balloon, he wanted to try it. Uncle Georgie groaned. "We can't move it back outside again," he explained. "I've got to get everything set for tomorrow."

"You're going to use it in the play, aren't you?" asked the president.

"Yes."

"You ought to try it out first, don't you think?"

"I guess we do need to show Peggy how to use it," said Georgie.

So that was how Peggy got to give the president a balloon ride. She would have been hopelessly embarrassed. But when Georgie explained to her how to make it go up and down, she had to pay attention to him and forget her shyness.

There was just enough room in the basket for her, the president, and the little stove that heated the air that made the balloon rise. The stove was already lighted, and all they had to do was wait for the hot air to fill the balloon. Mr. Roosevelt gave her a big toothy smile. "Have you ever done this before?" he asked.

She shook her head.

"Well, neither have I," he said. "So you'll have to tell me if something goes wrong."

Just then, the balloon started to rise. It was a very odd feeling, and Peggy reached out for something to hold onto. It turned out to be the president's hand. She squeezed it tightly and then blushed. "I'm sorry," she said.

By now the balloon was completely off the stage and was going higher every second. "You know what I do when I feel afraid?" the president asked.

"No."

"I try to look right at what it is that's scaring me." With that, he lifted her up so she could look over the side of the basket. Everybody down below was staring up at them. Peggy laughed. It was the looks on their faces. They were more afraid than she was.

"Feel better?" he asked, as he lowered her back to the floor of the basket.

"Yes," Peggy replied.

"Then perhaps we should pay attention to where we're going. We must be about to hit the ceiling. Aren't you supposed to do something now?"

"Oh! I nearly forgot!" Peggy tugged at the cord that let some of the hot air out of the balloon. Immediately, she felt the basket stop rising. Then it started to fall again.

"Not too fast," the president cautioned her. She let go of the rope. The balloon steadied itself.

"It must be something you get the hang of," he said. "Like riding a horse. Do you ride?"

"Oh, yes," she said.

"Rather ride a horse than an automobile?" he asked with a grin.

She nodded, and he patted her hand. "So do I. Bring us back down now, gently. I have a secret service guard somewhere around, and he's probably nervous."

⊷═◐═⊷

There were so many guests that night that the Roosevelt children slept with Peggy, Jack, and Harry. Peggy shared her big canopy bed with

Ethel Roosevelt. As they crawled under the sheets, there was still a lot of noise coming from the boys' room down the hall.

"Did you lock the door?" Ethel asked.

"Why, no," said Peggy. "I never lock it."

"The boys *might* raid us," Ethel said. "Although it's much more likely that they'll attack Papa."

"Attack the president? Doesn't he have a guard?"

Ethel giggled. "I only mean they'll rush his room and have a pillow fight. They almost always do in the White House."

Peggy lay back on the pillow and tried to imagine that. "Really?" she said. "Doesn't he have a lot of work to do? I mean, in running the country."

"Papa has a lot of energy," Ethel said.

The noise down the hall suddenly ceased. "Get ready now," Ethel said. "That means they're planning something. I'd lock the door if I were you."

"Jack and Harry wouldn't burst into my room at night," Peggy said.

"You don't know my brothers," Ethel said. "They once smuggled a pony into the White House and put it in my room."

Peggy was curious. She got out of bed and tiptoed toward the door. She put her ear to it and listened. She could hear faint whispering and cries of "shush!" but they didn't seem to be right outside.

Carefully, she turned the knob and opened the door without making a sound. She peeked around the edge of the door and saw the boys going down the hall toward the other wing. Just as Ethel had said, they were all carrying pillows.

Peggy turned and said, "I think I'm going to follow them. Want to come along?"

"Oh, no," Ethel said. "I'm warning you. They won't hold back just because you're a girl. You'll be positively pummeled with pillows."

Peggy had no time to answer, because just then she heard a terrifying roar from down the hall. She saw Mr. Roosevelt jump out from behind a marble statue, swinging a pillow. Shrieks of terror and laughter followed as the boys ran back toward their room, pursued by the president.

Peggy slammed the door and turned the lock. She stood with her back to it, listening to the noise of the pillow fighting. "I saw the president . . . in his nightshirt!" she said.

"If you know what's good for you," Ethel said, "you'll get some sleep. Because he's likely to bang on our door early in the morning to make us go on an obstacle hike. And he may be in his nightshirt then, too."

Peggy didn't even *ask* what an obstacle hike might be.

She found out soon enough. As Ethel predicted, her father pounded on the children's doors soon after the sun appeared. Peggy was ready. A few minutes earlier, she had slipped out of bed without awakening Ethel. She poked her head out the door.

Mr. Roosevelt seemed surprised. "You're an early riser," he said.

"When you've tasted Bridget's breakfast, you'll know why," she told him.

Bridget was ready. This was her chance to cook for the president, and she wasn't going to waste it. Besides the usual stack of hotcakes, she made two kinds of sausages, breakfast steak, eggs both scrambled and sunny-side up, in addition to hot cereal, biscuits, blueberry muffins, and toast. To top all of that off, she set out butter, maple syrup, wild honey, and several kinds of preserves, jams, and marmalade.

The amazing thing was that after the Roosevelt children came downstairs, every bit of food was eaten. Peggy kept reminding herself that it wasn't polite to stare. She'd never seen anybody put away food like the Roosevelts.

And then Mr. Roosevelt said, "Who's ready for an obstacle hike?"

As it turned out, to go on an obstacle hike you chose a place you wanted to hike to. Then you had to go there in a straight line. You couldn't go around obstacles like rocks or ponds or buildings. You had to climb over them, swim them, or some-how get through them. Whatever obstacle got in your way, you had to overcome it.

Jack and Harry had already heard about the hike from the Roosevelt boys. They'd picked out a destination—the new theater. There was a perfectly good road that led around the house, past the lake, and into the little glen where the theater was. But the whole idea of the obstacle hike was *not* to use the ordinary roads or paths.

No danger of that, Peggy thought as she helped Ethel climb out the window of an empty stall in the barn. The straight line between the house and the theater just happened to go through there. It also led across a stream. Fortunately, it was frozen, although Quentin and Jack both fell on the ice. Then up a hill where a covering of snow hid a hole that Archie stepped in and twisted his ankle. Going down the hill on the other side, both Peggy and Ethel slipped on some rotting leaves and skidded into a tree at the bottom.

"You aren't supposed to complain," Ethel whispered to Peggy as they picked themselves up. Peggy was out of breath, and didn't reply. But she thought to herself that she'd be grateful if she lived through the hike.

They stopped for a discussion when they reached a large old oak tree. Was it fair to go around it, or should they climb it?

"If we climbed it," Jack pointed out, "we'd just have to climb down again."

"Well, of course you'd climb down on the other *side* of the tree," said Kermit. But Mr. Roosevelt decided that it was all right to step around it if you held onto the tree while doing it.

With a great deal of relief, Peggy saw the theater up ahead. They'd already spent over an hour and a half getting there, when it would have taken them less than ten minutes by the road. Of course, the injuries had slowed them down a bit. By now, even Mr. Roosevelt had a scrape on his head where he'd forgotten to duck under a rocky ledge. He had tied a handkerchief around his forehead, making him look a little like a pirate himself–if pirates wore glasses.

However, one final obstacle lay between them and the theater.

Mr. Pomeroy's Packard automobile.

It was parked on the other side of the wooden fence that surrounded the theater. Peggy looked around, but there was no sign of Mr. Pomeroy.

Meanwhile, the others were climbing the fence, which had metal loops in the top for people to hitch their horses to. She followed, joining the others who were looking at the Packard.

"Is this your family's automobile?" asked Mr. Roosevelt.

Jack and Harry laughed. "No, it belongs to somebody who owns a store in town."

"I suppose we could crawl under it," said Mr. Roosevelt. He stooped down. "Not a lot of room for me, although Quentin and Archie should have no trouble."

"We could just climb into the front seat and march through," Harry pointed out.

"Do you know the fellow well?" asked Mr. Roosevelt. "I'm afraid our shoes are a bit snowy and muddy."

"Oh, we know him quite well," Jack replied innocently. "He's a good-humored sort of person. Anyway, he doesn't seem to be around."

That was *one* true thing Jack said, thought Peggy. She wondered where Mr. Pomeroy had gone. Anyway, Jack had already lifted himself into the front of the Packard and stepped down on the other side. Quickly, the others followed, with the president bringing up the rear.

"Hey!" A shout of surprise and anger came at them from the side of the theater.

Mr. Pomeroy came running toward them, shaking his fist. "What are you kids doing in my automobile?" he yelled.

As he approached, Mr. Roosevelt stepped in front of the children. "It's entirely my fault, sir," he started to explain.

Mr. Pomeroy hardly glanced at him. He had his eyes on Jack and Harry and wanted revenge. "Look at your boots!" he was shouting. "You've ruined my automobile."

"Oh, I think it can be cleaned up," Mr. Roosevelt said. "I hope you'll accept my apologies."

Mr. Pomeroy whirled and looked at him at last. Well, Mr. Roosevelt *did* have a handkerchief wrapped around his head, but Peggy thought Mr. Pomeroy should have recognized him. After all his picture was in the newspapers nearly every day.

He didn't though. Not right away. "Who do you think you're dealing with?" Mr. Pomeroy shouted.

The president lifted his head a little and looked at Mr. Pomeroy through his eyeglasses. "I don't think we've met," he said. Then he gave that big, toothy grin, stuck out his hand and said, "I'm Theodore Roosevelt."

It took a second for that to sink into Mr. Pomeroy's angry brain. Then his jaw dropped slowly. It dropped a long way. "You're . . . you're the *president*," he said.

"I didn't catch your name," said Mr. Roosevelt, still holding out his hand.

Mr. Pomeroy suddenly realized it was there and grabbed it. "Samuel Pomeroy," he said, shaking the president's hand as if he were pumping water from a well. "Sam, really," he said, trying to smile, "to my friends."

"Pleased to meet you, Sam," said the president, trying to get his hand back. "I think we can find some way to clean your automobile."

Mr. Pomeroy looked at the automobile. "Oh, yes, not to worry," he said. He still held the president's hand, and now pulled him closer. He leaned over to speak quietly into Mr. Roosevelt's ear. "Are you here to inspect the theater?" he asked.

"Oh, no," said Mr. Roosevelt. "I'm a guest of the Aldriches."

Mr. Pomeroy seemed shocked. He finally let go of the president's hand. "But, sir," he said. "Did you know that they're actors?"

"Why, certainly," said the president. "Who hasn't seen Lionel, Adele, or their children on the stage?"

Mr. Pomeroy drew himself up straight. "I'm sure I haven't," he said.

"Oh, no? Well, you should come by tomorrow and attend the performance," said the president. "It's free, after all."

Mr. Pomeroy seemed distressed. "It may be dangerous," he warned.

"How so?"

"There may be violations of fire regulations."

The president nodded gravely. "I'll be on the lookout for them."

Mr. Pomeroy shook his head. He murmured, "The president staying at an actor's house. What is the country coming to?" He got into his car and drove off.

"A strange man," said the president when Mr. Pomeroy left. "He didn't seem to want us to clean his automobile."

ELEVEN

The Pirates Make a Lot of Mistakes

DECEMBER 31, 1902

THEY REHEARSED FOR THE REST OF THE MORNING. Rehearsal was just the way Peggy had remembered it—a lot of standing around and watching. Still, when her turn on stage came, she never had any trouble remembering her lines.

Bridget brought over a nice lunch for everyone, and once more the Roosevelts attacked as if they hadn't eaten for a week. Peggy sat next to Mr. Roosevelt on the deck of the pirate ship.

"Isn't watching the rehearsal boring for you?" she asked.

"Not at all," he said. "I was in the Hasty Pudding Club at Harvard. That's the drama group, you see. I've always enjoyed the theater."

133

"I'm sure Grandpa would write a part for you in this play if you wanted," she said.

He shook his head. "There would be too much of a fuss about that," he told her. "I want to sit in the best seat in the house and enjoy myself."

By late afternoon, Grandpa decided that they all knew their parts well enough. "Get some rest. Take a nap if you like. We'll have a light supper before the performance. You can eat more at the party afterward." He looked sternly at the children. "But anyone who forgets a line won't be allowed into the party."

Peggy and the boys assured the Roosevelt children that Grandpa was only joking. As they walked back to the house, they saw people already arriving for the performance. Several carriages and buggies passed them. A few people were walking up the driveway from the front gate.

"That's a good sign," said Jack.

"I guess since admission is free, they came early to get good seats," Peggy said.

"Or maybe they're coming because they heard the president is here," Harry suggested.

"Papa didn't tell anyone until the last minute," Teddy Jr. said. "I'm sure the reporters don't know. He hates to be followed about."

-+===0◐===+-

Two hours later, they were all back in the theater again. Peggy peeked out through the curtains. The house was packed. Grandpa would be so pleased.

As she watched, President Roosevelt entered the front box just to the left of the stage. Murmurs of excitement spread through the audience as people recognized him.

A minute later, the house lights dimmed. Grandpa called out, "Places, everyone!" and the curtain opened. Peggy was in the first scene, along with Ethel Roosevelt, Polly, Molly, Freddy, and Nell. They were going to be the innocent children who were kidnapped. Peggy was surprised at how bright the electric footlights were. Even so, she could see the first few rows of the audience. People seemed to be enjoying themselves.

Soon, the pirates arrived. Peggy and the others were scooped up and taken aboard the pirate ship. The ship itself was one of the most impressive pieces of scenery in the play. It had been set up to actually move across the stage. In the background were the smaller ships that were supposed to be left burning as the pirates left the harbor. Grandpa had planned this to be an exciting climax to the first act.

Though Peggy had been tied up by the pirates, she could see what the audience could not. In the wings, Grandpa had finally given Jack the potassium. Dressed in his pirate costume, Jack was going to use it to set the ships on fire.

Just as soon as he dropped the potassium into the water, Peggy began to worry. It burst into flame, just as Jack had said it would. The flames were a lovely color, violet and bright yellow mixed together. But they seemed to be higher than Peggy had expected. Even Jack jumped back a little.

The footlights had been darkened especially for this scene, to make the flames appear even brighter. As a result, Peggy and the other actors could see the people in the front rows clearly. Their faces lit up in delight, as if they were watching a fireworks display.

Meanwhile, Jack was running along the row of flaming ships, waving his arms at somebody in the wings. A worried stagehand had decided the fire was getting out of hand. Before Jack could stop him, he tossed a bucket of water over the flames.

Whoosh! It was like throwing kerosene on a pile of burning leaves. The fire made a thumping sound and reached higher up, toward the draperies in back of the stage. "Sand," Jack called to the stagehands. "Sand will stop it."

Nobody in the audience could hear him, fortunately. Everybody thought the runaway fire was part of the play, and the audience was applauding and cheering. Meanwhile, the pirate ship moved in front of the fire. Several stagehands ran out to throw sand on the roaring flames, and they started to die down. Peggy heard Grandpa order, "Curtain!" and down it came. She could still hear the people out front cheering.

Harry looked down at Peggy. "Wasn't that *great?*" he asked.

"Harry," she said, "Jack almost burned the theater down."

"Oh, no," Harry said. "Jack was just having fun, that's all."

⋆⟶⟹⟸⋆

The second act went a bit more smoothly. Most of the children weren't on stage for it. The adults, playing their parents, found out they'd been kidnapped and organized a rescue. Aunt Laura got to sing a couple of songs that really didn't have much to do with the plot. But she sang so well that Grandpa had to write them in.

Backstage, Jack was checking the burn holes in his costume. Peggy told him, "You know, I was tied up with ropes. If you had burned down the theater I couldn't have escaped."

"Oh, Harry would have saved you," he said. "He wouldn't have missed the chance to be a hero."

"Where is he anyway?" she asked. "He should be getting ready for the sword fight."

"He is," Jack replied. "He's watching Father from the wings."

Here came Harry now, but he looked worried for some reason.

"Jack," he said, "do you remember that man on the train?"

"What man?"

"Last summer, when we were coming up from New York. The one who stole the wallet."

Jack stopped brushing the soot off his costume. "Oh, the one *you* saw," he said. "Yes, and then I had to turn my pockets out and open my suitcase, as if I were—"

"I think he's here," Harry interrupted.

"What do you mean, here?"

"When your fire was going, I saw somebody in the audience. I couldn't think who he was until a few minutes ago. Then I went and looked from the wings. He's in the third row, left center, aisle seat."

Jack shook his head. "How could you remember him from that long ago?"

"He pushed his way past me on the train," Harry said. "His face was right next to mine."

Jack shrugged. "Well, you can't do anything about it now. Even if it is him."

"We should keep an eye on him," said Harry. He turned to Peggy. "Will you try to watch him while you're on stage? He has a sandy mustache."

Peggy agreed.

"Especially when you're up in the balloon," Harry said. "You should have a good view from there."

However, when the balloon scene finally came, Peggy had a lot of other things to think about. It had been easier rehearsing with President Roosevelt. Now she had Freddy and Nell in the basket with her, and they kept trying to lean over the sides of the basket. Peggy had to hold onto them with one hand and control the hot-air rope with the other.

The audience loved the scene, however. They oohed and aahed when the colorful balloon rose into the air. Grandpa had dimmed the lights again, letting spotlights play against the sides of the air bag. Ribbons streamed from the sides of the basket. As Freddy and Nell peeped over the side, they waved at the audience, which made everybody laugh. Up they went, until the balloon finally disappeared from the audience's view.

The curtain fell. Now Peggy had to keep Freddy and Nell from fidgeting while the scenery was changed. It was spooky up here in the rafters, without being able to see the audience. Suddenly the balloon began to sink toward the stage. Peggy turned and saw that Nell had pulled the cord that let air out of the balloon.

Peggy grabbed the cord away, and Nell began to cry. Not knowing why, Freddy started to cry, too. The balloon was still falling, and Peggy frantically opened the vent on the stove. It was supposed to heat the air and make the balloon rise. But it wasn't doing it fast enough. As the balloon hurtled downward, some of the stagehands looked up and began to shout.

Whoever was in charge of the curtain thought that was the signal to raise it. The audience didn't notice the stagehands scattering to get out of the way. They were gasping as they saw that the balloon was about to crash. Peggy put her arms around Nell and Freddy and braced herself.

But there was no crash, only a little bump as the balloon reached the stage. Luckily, the stove had heated the air just enough to break their fall. "Get out, get out!" Peggy whispered to the children.

Nell shook her head stubbornly. "Flag," she said.

Oh, yes. Peggy had forgotten. In Grandpa's script, the two babies were supposed to get out of the basket waving American flags. "What's a flag doing in the balloon?" Peggy had asked during rehearsal.

"No one will worry about that," said Grandpa. "Anytime you want to get a cheer, just wave the flag."

And he was right, as usual. When Nell and Freddy stepped out of the basket waving their little flags, the audience roared. The people thought that the near-crash of the balloon was just another stunt. People stood and applauded for so long that Peggy was embarrassed. But she looked down and saw that Nell's eyes were bright as she waved her flag as hard as she could.

When they finally marched into the wings, Grandpa was there. He patted Nell on the head and said, "She's an Aldrich, all right."

Harry was there, too, and stopped Peggy. "Did you see him?" he asked.

"See who?" She had completely forgotten.

"The man in the third row, left center, aisle seat."

"Harry, I'm sorry, I didn't have time to look."

He shook his head in disgust. "This man could be a thief. He might be worse," he said darkly. "President Lincoln was shot in a theater, you know."

"Do you think this man has a gun?" asked Peggy.

"You never can tell," replied Harry. He stalked off.

"If you think it's so easy, try watching him when you're on stage," Peggy called after him. But he didn't hear her.

Harry's big scene was coming up next. Although Peggy, Freddy, and Nell had escaped, Polly and Molly and Ethel were still lost on Pirate Island. Heroic Uncle Richard was leading a rescue party by sea. As Richard's ship moved onto the stage, the pirates boarded their ship and headed the other way. Uncle Richard leaped onto the pirate ship, drawing his sword. Harry, as the pirate chieftain, swung down on a rope to meet him.

Peggy watched from the wings. It was an exciting fight. Harry had learned quite a few tricks from Grandpa. He leaped backwards, switched the sword from one hand to the other, and even kept fighting when he slipped and fell onto the deck.

Uncle Richard was having a fine time, too. He didn't have to do spectacular tricks. He just moved so smoothly and looked so good that people loved to watch him. Peggy saw him smile a few times, whenever Harry made a particularly good move. He even let Harry upstage him! Peggy watched in horror as Harry moved toward the rear of the stage so that Uncle Richard had to turn his back on the audience. You were never supposed to do that to a star.

Harry hoped that his father didn't mind being upstaged. He had only wanted to move to a spot where he could look into the audience. So he'd jumped onto the pilot's deck of the ship, where the steering wheel was. From here, he was a little taller than his father, and could keep him at bay while he checked the man in the third row.

And as Harry peered beyond the footlights, he spotted the man again. For some reason, the man wasn't watching the stage. Harry strained his eyes. He was getting out of his seat! The man ducked to avoid blocking the view of those behind him as he slipped into the aisle.

Harry was probably the only person in the theater to notice. Everybody else's eyes were glued to the stage, watching the sword fight. Harry gritted his teeth. He wouldn't let the man escape a second time. He shouted, "Stop that man!"

Naturally, everybody in the theater was completely astonished. What did the pirate mean by that? Even Harry's father stared at him in surprise. "That man!" Harry called, pointing up the aisle with his sword.

Still, nobody understood. Harry grabbed a rope that was hanging from the rigging of the ship. Sticking the blade of his sword between his teeth, he took a flying leap off the pilot's deck and swung way out over the footlights. Below him, the audience looked up in amazement. Then he let go.

Oof! Harry landed in the aisle harder than he'd expected to, and fell to his knees. He got up and rushed up the aisle, where the man was struggling into his coat. Harry caught him by the sleeve, and pulled him back.

By this time, the audience was buzzing. Was this part of the play? Nobody knew. The man wriggled free, and Harry hit him with his sword. But that only annoyed him, because of course it wasn't a real one.

Then a high-pitched voice rang out from the boxes above the main floor. "Someone hold that man!" All eyes went to the president, who was pointing to where Harry and the man were struggling. Almost at once, they were surrounded by people who'd gotten out of their seats.

And then came another voice. "Hey! I think my wallet's been stolen!" With a sigh of relief, Harry looked and saw that it was the man next to the vacant seat where the sandy-haired man had been sitting.

"Look in his pockets," Harry said. "I know this man is a thief."

TWELVE

Curtain Call

IT TOOK A WHILE TO GET THINGS BACK ON TRACK (or on boat), but they did finish the play. The wallet was found, the thief was taken to jail, and Harry had to die (on stage). But the audience gave him a tremendous round of applause, because they knew he was really a hero after all.

Grandpa got carried away when the cast and author took their third curtain call, and invited everybody in the audience to come up to the house for a party. Bridget nearly fainted when she heard.

Fortunately, most of the audience had their own New Year's Eve parties to go to. But a lot of

145

people stopped by just to shake Grandpa's hand—and the president's, too. Some of them even clapped Harry on the back.

Eventually, things returned to normal. That meant that there were only about a dozen children running through the house, sliding down the curved marble banister, or playing the new indoor sport of Ping-Pong that someone had received for Christmas. Some of the adults wanted to try it, too.

Peggy brought Mr. Roosevelt a platter of oysters. They had been caught in the ocean that morning. He slurped one down while watching the Ping-Pong game.

"Can I ask you a question?" Peggy said. "In the theater, why did you call out for somebody to grab the thief? Nobody else in the audience knew what Harry was up to."

"Well, I certainly didn't," he replied. "But I'd seen him on the obstacle hike, and that told me all I needed to know."

"On the obstacle hike?"

"You see, the obstacle hike is not just a hike," said Mr. Roosevelt.

"I certainly learned *that*," said Peggy. She was still sore from sliding down the hill on her bottom.

"In life," the president said, "we run into all sorts of obstacles. The idea is to keep heading toward our goals no matter what tries to stop us. That's what the hike is all about. And Harry caught on right away. He didn't let anything get in his way."

Peggy felt confused. "So . . . "

"So I could see that Harry *must* have had a reason for jumping into the audience. Either it was a very unusual scene in the play, or he was onto something that no one else could see." Mr. Roosevelt slurped down another oyster, and Peggy saw that he'd now had six. "I had confidence in him."

"Well, I'm glad you did," Peggy said.

The younger children started to fall asleep on the floor or in chairs. Somebody fell off the banister and began to cry. Annie took them upstairs, one by one, and put them to bed. Nell was the last to go, and Peggy remembered the night she was born, exactly three years ago. It was true what Mama said—time went by so quickly.

Mr. Roosevelt said to the boys, "Who's up for a pillow fight?" They all roared with delight and scrambled up the stairs.

Ethel sat down on the couch next to Peggy. "That's his way of getting them to go to bed," she said. "Mama says he wears them out. But I would like to stay up for the new year, wouldn't you?"

"Yes," said Peggy. "I've done it every year since the turn of the century."

"I envy you," Ethel said suddenly.

Peggy was surprised. "Why?" she asked.

"Oh, it must be so interesting to live here."

"Boring is more like it," said Peggy.

"How can you say that?"

"I would much rather be on the road acting with Mama and Papa."

"Well," Ethel replied after a moment, "you can act here, now that you have a theater. And as for travel . . . I went on a campaign trip with Papa once. It was so tiring, because you didn't even know what city you were in."

"Do you go to school?" Peggy asked.

Ethel was surprised. "Of course," she said. "Papa wouldn't allow any of his children not to be educated."

"I think I'm ready to be educated," Peggy said. Yes, she realized. That was right. She'd tell Mama tomorrow. Maybe she could go away to a boarding school for girls, just for a year to see if she liked it.

Grandma interrupted them. "Peggy," she said. "Have you seen your grandfather?"

"Not in a while," Peggy replied.

"He wouldn't want to miss the new year," Grandma said. "Will you go up and see if he's fallen asleep in the study?"

Peggy went up the staircase, smiling as she thought of what Grandpa would say when she told him she wanted to go to school. She opened the door to his office and saw him asleep in the leather chair behind his cherrywood desk. He looked very peaceful. A smile was on his face as if he were dreaming of something happy. Maybe it was the success of his play.

Something else caught her eye then. His pocket watch sat on the desk, but its cover was standing open. The music wasn't playing.

The song had ended.

PEGGY SAT WRAPPED UP IN HER QUILT, LOOKING out the window. She didn't know if she was allowed to come into Grandpa's study anymore. But all the adults were downstairs, so no one would care. She could hear them talking. They had been very upset the past few days.

It was February now, and Grandpa had been dead for a month. Peggy had a little stack of photographs she had taken at the memorial service. A lot of famous actors had been there—Edwin Booth, John Drew, Maud Adams, and many others. At some point, Peggy would paste all the pictures into an album for Grandma.

Grandma had kept everyone's spirits up. She said that Grandpa had finished his career just the way he wanted to. That was true, Peggy thought. He wrote his own play and saw his children and grandchildren on stage in his own theater. Everything had been just the way he wanted.

Was that why he died? She wondered. Maybe you try and try to get things just right, and when you do . . . that's the end.

The voices from downstairs had gotten louder. Harry and Jack had gone back to school, but Uncle Richard and Aunt Laura were still here. Papa was here, too, along with Uncle Nick. They should have been out on tour somewhere, acting. Even Uncle Georgie was in the room downstairs, trying to explain something. Everybody shushed him, as usual.

Peggy started to listen. They had been looking for something ever since the week after Grandpa died. She didn't know what. Now, she overheard the real problem. It was Mr. Pomeroy again, no surprise there. He had hired a lawyer to prove that the Aldriches didn't own the land where Grandpa had built the house and theater.

That was silly, of course. Just something mean that Mr. Pomeroy would do. If Grandpa didn't own the land, why didn't somebody stop him from building there? The person who owned it would have said something.

But it didn't seem to be as simple as that. Now the Aldriches had to show a deed, a paper of some kind. And they couldn't find Grandpa's will, either. That was what everybody had been looking for. They had gone through all the drawers in Grandpa's desk, the filing cabinets he kept in the study, his theater trunks. Nobody could find the deed or the will.

Peggy understood now. She traced her initials on the window, thinking. Peggy was just a nickname, of course. Her real name was Elizabeth. E.A. Maybe if she was a famous actress someday—

Then it came to her. Grandpa, she asked. Why didn't you tell anybody where you hid your papers? I'll bet I know where they are.

But if I find them, Peggy thought, maybe I'll have to live here forever. If I *don't* tell anybody where the papers are, then Mama and Papa will have to go out and act again. They'll take me and Nell along, and we'll have fun, just like before.

She thought about that for a moment, and then shook her head. Grandma would have to leave the house, too. Mr. Pomeroy would win. Everything that Grandpa had built would be destroyed.

Peggy could stop that. She was the only one who could. And after all, she was an Aldrich. So she had to do it.

She sighed and went through the curtains that were drawn around the window seat. The study seemed darker and duller now that Grandpa wasn't here anymore. The posters already looked a little faded and dusty.

She walked to the other end of the room, to the place where she remembered Grandpa had been. On New Year's Eve when the house was filled with smoke. She lifted up the corner of the carpet. It was hard to find a floorboard that was loose. She had to pick at each one with her fingernails, but finally one lifted up.

Peggy saw the leather case that Grandpa had taken with him when he thought the house was on fire. She looked inside. There were sheets of paper, with seals and signatures at the bottom. She recognized Grandpa's signature. It was a fancy signature, dramatic and bold. Sad to think that nobody would ever sign his name that way again.

Peggy began to imagine how she would go downstairs now. Walking very slowly. Holding the case in both hands. When she entered the room where all the adults were, she would say something that would make them pay attention. Something very dramatic.

She had learned how from Grandpa.

A Few Historical Notes

The word *cunning* today means "crafty" or "sly." At the turn of the century, it was a slang word meaning just about the same thing as the slang word *cool* today.

The curved-dashboard Oldsmobile was one of the most popular of the early automobiles. The body really was made of wood, not metal. Ransom Olds, who designed and built it, sold 2,500 cars in 1902—more than any other automaker of the time. The Oldsmobile cost $650. It was probably the first automobile ever to be the subject of a song—"In My Merry Oldsmobile." However, that song was written in 1904, so we didn't put it into our story. We didn't have Uncle Georgie store the Oldsmobile in a garage, because that word didn't appear in English until a little later.

Theodore Roosevelt became president by accident. In 1900, the Republican party nominated him as vice president. He hadn't wanted to be vice president, for he was already governor of New York State. But a political boss in New York wanted to get rid of Roosevelt because he was too honest and eager to fight corruption. However, less than a year after the election, President William McKinley was assassinated. Theodore Roosevelt, at age forty-two, became the youngest president in United States history.

Roosevelt really did treat his children the way we have portrayed in our story—pillow fights and obstacle hikes included. If you read *Theodore Roosevelt's Letters to His Children*, and *Letters to Kermit*, by Theodore Roosevelt, you will discover what a lively place the White House was in those years.

155

The Aldrich

Lionel (1833–1902)

m

 m

 m

Richard (1866–)   Laura (1867–)   William (1867–)   Anna (1868–)

Harry (1887–)   Jack (1888–)   Peggy (1889–)   Nell (1900–)

Family

Adele (1838–)

Zena (1840–)

Maud (1872–)

m

Nick Woods (1870–)

George (1874–)

Molly (1898–)

Polly (1898–)

Freddy (1899–)

Things That Really Happened

The 1900 census recorded almost 76 million people living in the United States. There were 1,335,911 telephones, and about 8,000 automobiles.

At the beginning of the decade, the average American worker earned 22 cents an hour, and worked a 59-hour week.

1900

The Wizard of Oz, by L. Frank Baum, is published.

Hershey chocolate bars are first sold.

A hurricane kills 6,000 people in Galveston, Texas, on September 8.

1901

New York City police arrest a group of actors for appearing in costume on a Sunday.

On September 6, President William McKinley is shot at a fair in Buffalo, NY, and died eight days later. Theodore Roosevelt, at 42, becomes the youngest U.S. president.

1902

Ragtime music becomes popular. Its most famous composer was Scott Joplin.

Morris Michtom, a New York toymaker, sold the first Teddy bears, named after the president of the United States.

Ping-Pong, invented in Britain, becomes a fad in the United States.

Ida Tarbell begins writing a series of articles about the ruthless and unfair business practices of the Standard Oil Company. Later published as a book, Tarbell's work caused a public outcry. In 1911, the U.S. Supreme Court ordered the company to be broken up so it would not be so powerful.

During the Years 1900–1909

1903

Movie theaters show *The Great Train Robbery,* the first American movie to tell a story.

An automobile completes the first transcontinental trip, leaving San Francisco on May 23 and arriving in New York City on July 26.

The first baseball World Series is held. In a best-of-nine series, Boston of the American League beat Pittsburgh of the National League five games to three.

On December 17, at Kitty Hawk, North Carolina, Orville and Wilbur Wright fly their invention, the first successful airplane.

1904

The ice-cream cone is invented at the St. Louis World's Fair.

Henry Ford sets a land-speed record in an automobile of 91.37 miles per hour.

New York becomes the first state to pass speed limits: 10 miles per hour in cities, and 20 miles an hour in rural areas.

1905

The Chicago & North Western becomes the first railroad to install electric lights on its cars.

1906

On April 18, a severe earthquake strikes San Francisco. Along with fires that followed, the disaster left 250,000 people homeless, destroyed 25,000 buildings, and killed around 500.

Kellogg's Corn Flakes are sold for the first time.

Upton Sinclair's novel *The Jungle* becomes a best-seller. It exposes horrible conditions in the meatpacking industry.

Congress passes a law requiring government inspection of meat-packing plants.

1907

Oklahoma becomes the 46th state.

1908

Henry Ford's automobile company introduces the Model T. It would become the first low-priced car, and the price went lower almost every year. It sold until 1928, for a total of about 15 million cars, making it the most popular automobile in the world.

William Howard Taft is elected president. Weighing over 300 pounds, he was the heaviest president, and once got stuck in the White House bathtub.

1909

Congress passes the 16th Amendment to the Constitution, allowing the federal government to tax the incomes of its citizens. The amendment was ratified by the states in 1913.

There are about 8,000 movie theaters in the United States. Admission is a nickel, giving them the name "nickelodeons."

The National Association for the Advancement of Colored People (NAACP) is founded to promote legal rights for African Americans.